Who Can
You Trust?

Who Can You Trust?

by Chelsea Brooks

BOXTREE

First published in the UK 1994
by BOXTREE LIMITED
Broadwall House, 21 Broadwall, London SE1 9PL

First published in the USA 1993
by Collier Books
Macmillan Publishing Company
866 Third Avenue, New York, NY 10022

10 9 8 7 6 5 4 3 2 1

Printed and bound in Great Britain by
Cox and Wyman, Reading, Berkshire

A catalogue record for this book is available from the British Library

ISBN 0 7522 0911 6

To
the wonderful cast
of "California
Dreams"

Chapter 1

Sharkey's, the best beachside hangout around, was loaded with kids as Sly Winkle sat down at one of the center tables. He looked around, scoping out all the cute girls as he listened to the music blasting from the jukebox.

"Not bad," Sly muttered, grimacing a little. The group playing was a plastic copy of a *real* band. He recognized them as a California-based group that was currently zooming up the charts. "Tinker and the Bells," he snorted. "They're nowhere near as good of a band as California Dreams is."

"Did you say something, Winkle?" a gruff voice demanded behind Sly's right shoulder.

Sly turned around. Sharkey himself, owner and resident grouch, walked over and flicked a towel across Sly's table. This, apparently, was Sharkey's answer to deep cleaning. Sly knew that his friend Tony Wicks, who worked for Sharkey, would be called in later to clean up the tables.

"I was talking about the music. Bubble gum music," Sly clarified. "You know, the kind that sticks to your gums. The kind of music you are currently promoting in this fine eating establishment."

"Uh-huh." Sharkey looked bored.

Sly got up and put his arm around Sharkey, gesturing broadly with his free hand. "Picture this: Huge crowds. Lots of orders. Money rolling in. And all because you hired California Dreams on a steady basis. Not to mention the fact that your taste in music would improve."

Honoring Sharkey with his most appealing, charming, and decimating smile, Sly expected instant agreement from the belligerent, egg-shaped man. Sure, Sharkey had a face only a mother could love and a Godzilla-like attitude, but the guy was really a pushover. Really.

Sharkey leaned down to him, nose-to-nose. "If I wanted a band, Winkle, I'd hire the Beatles."

"Sharkey, I hate to be the one to break it to you, but they broke up years ago."

"No kidding. Now, why don't you make like a banana and split. You're taking up valuable space in *my* restaurant." With that, he headed toward the kitchen.

"Hey, I ordered a Shark burger," Sly yelled. "You want me to take my business elsewhere?"

Sharkey stopped and pretended to consider. "Depends on whether you plan on paying this time," he chortled, and then herded his bulk behind the counter and into the kitchen.

Sly made a face. Well, okay, he *had* forgotten to pay the check a time or two, but it wasn't like he was a criminal or anything. Every time it had been because Sharkey had owed the Dreams some money, and Sly, as manager of the band, had been owed his portion of the settlement as well. So he'd taken payment in food. So what? That's the way Sharkey always paid them.

And besides, was it his fault that the last time California Dreams had played here things had gotten a little out of hand? No way! Well, not really, anyway. Sharkey *had* owed them money even if he hadn't felt they deserved it. What a cheapskate! Why, it was plain stupid to come here and take this abuse!

I oughtta be really upset! Sly thought, working himself up to righteous indignation.

Except . . .

Maybe he had been a little at fault. Just a little. And, after all, Sharkey's was *the* establishment to hang out in. No reason for him to make a rash decision just because Sharkey had blamed him for that unfortunate incident that was *not* his fault.

3

Besides, Tony worked here, and Tony was one of his friends.

At that very moment, Tony swept in from the kitchen, balancing three plates of burgers and fries. He stopped, bumped one to Sly across the table with his hip, then sailed over to the next table where he deftly shot two plates, Frisbee-like, across the tabletop, one to each of the waiting bikini-clad girls.

"Cool!" the first girl declared as her plate slid right to the edge of the table in front of her.

"Wow." The other one blinked in amazement.

"That's right, ladies." Tony flashed them a grin, proudly displaying his Sharkey's uniform, an aqua baseball shirt worn by all Sharkey's employees. "This is no ordinary waiter you see before you. And that"—he indicated his deft plate-sliding move—"that's the world-famous Wicks-slick-and-tricky-counter-slip-and-slide-to-your-mouth-in-your-eyes burger and fries!"

"Cool!" the first girl said again, pouring ketchup onto the mound of fries.

"Tony." Sly gestured his friend to take the chair next to his.

"Don't go away. I'll be right back," Tony promised his newfound friends. "What?" he asked Sly as he flipped a chair around backward and straddled it. "And make it quick. There's work to be done." He glanced back at the girls and smiled.

"I think Sharkey's weakening. The last time

California Dreams played here, the place was packed. He's going to ask us back. I can feel it."

Tony stared at Sly through astonished brown eyes. "No way, man! Have you forgotten what happened last time the Dreams tuned up on that stage?"

"Ummm . . ." Sly munched on a fry and glanced around to see if anyone was listening. He hated reviewing past mistakes.

"In case your brain's tuned into super slow, man, let me refresh your memory. Last time we played, someone spread the rumor that Jason Priestley was going to be here. Then there was a major mob scene over some guy with sideburns. We were lucky that the few bucks Sharkey intended to pay us covered the cost of those two broken chairs!" Tony narrowed his gaze at his friend. "I can't imagine who could have started that rumor."

"Don't look at me." Sly quickly backtracked. "We're lucky Sharkey even allows us *in* here."

"Tony, that is history. We've got to think of the present. I know I can strike a deal with Sharkey. He said, and I quote, 'The only band I want here more than California Dreams is the Beatles.'"

"The Beatles ain't going to play here," Tony pointed out. "You might be manager of the band, but you are brain dead about music!"

"I know about the Beatles!" Sly snapped.

5

"Now pay attention. This is important."

"You've got two minutes."

Sly started talking fast. He needed Tony to be with him on this. Yeah, okay, he'd started the Jason Priestley rumor and the Dreams had all been burned at him, but, hey, it had gotten people to come to Sharkey's, didn't it?

"Matt's writing a new song," Sly reminded Tony. "It'll positively herd 'em in. Sharkey'll make big bucks this time. Big bucks. And that means we'll make big bucks, too."

"Nice try." Tony shoved his chair back when he saw Sharkey returning from the kitchen, and then Tony hurried to look busy, listening intently to the order of another customer.

Sly munched thoughtfully on his Shark burger. He *had* to convince Sharkey to bring California Dreams back. It was the only way to redeem himself in Jenny Garrison's eyes. Ever since that last fiasco, she'd stopped speaking to him, and that was saying a lot, since Jenny had the second-fastest mouth at Pacific Coast High, Tony's being the uncontested first.

Sly sighed. *What's wrong with Jenny?* he asked himself. *Why can't she see what she's missing? I'm the coolest. The best. The man for her.*

For a moment he envisioned slim, dark-haired Jenny in his arms, her sparkling brown eyes, her cynical smile, her arms surrounding him.

"Oh, Sly," she murmured. *"I've been so wrong. You are it, with a capital I, and I can't live without you one more microsecond!"*

The dream faded. Sly shook his head. He'd tried everything to make her see the truth. He'd even read her diary and turned himself into her "dream man." And it had almost worked, until she'd realized what he'd done. He'd *even* dated Jenny's best friend, Tiffani, for a while and had made himself believe *she* might be the girl for him. Wrong-o! It was Jenny all the way. After Tiffani had dumped him he had realized that.

Wait a minute. Back up. Reverse. Tiffani had *not* dumped the Sly-meister. They'd dumped each other. Actually, now that he thought about it, he must have dumped her. He'd just made sure she thought otherwise, because he didn't want to hurt her feelings.

But back to Jenny . . . Someone as insightful as Sylvester Winkle knew when he'd met the right girl. Jenny was *the* girl, and all he had to do was make sure she saw the soulful, sensitive guy in him beneath his sexy, handsome, totally manly exterior.

"Yeah," he said aloud, nodding. First on the agenda: to get Sharkey hot on California Dreams again.

Sly was getting to his feet when Tony suddenly came bouncing back from the kitchen. Sly could hear Sharkey yelling something from the other side of the swinging door.

"Whoa, man, the Shark's on a rampage," Tony revealed, casting a quick glance over his shoulder.

"Maybe this isn't a good time to approach him, huh?" Sly grimaced.

"Stay outta the way—and I mean outta the way!" Tony shook his head, running both hands over his short, curly black hair as if overwhelmed by a *major* problem. "He thinks I've been slacking off! Me!"

"Unbelievable." Sly managed to keep a straight face.

"He told me I have to serve X amount of tables per hour, and make sure I'm turning tables like that!" He snapped his fingers. "I've got to make ten bucks a table, per hour, as long as I'm working and not make anybody mad." He hesitated. "Does that sound like a math problem to you?"

Sly was still staring in the direction of the kitchen, where he could hear Sharkey's gruff voice above the sound of pots and pans being handled with less than baby-soft care. "I guess so."

"Man, I am the worst at math! How could he do this to me? I'm suffering with this subject enough at school!"

"Have you seen Jenny?" Sly asked.

"Aren't you listening to me?" Tony demanded, exasperated.

Sly patted him on the back. "Sure I am."

At that moment, Sharkey's front door opened and in walked Jenny herself. She was in the midst of what sounded like a major argument with her brother Matt. Jenny was talking a mile a minute and seemed upset. Matt was looking pretty mad himself.

Jenny practically slammed the door in Matt's face. "Women are equal to men!"

"I didn't say they weren't!" Matt, tall, brown haired and usually even tempered, shot a long-suffering glance Tony and Sly's way. Jenny was known for speaking her mind.

"You want me to take over your dishwashing job even though I'm on dinner detail this month. You think washing dishes is women's work," Jenny accused.

"Wait a minute." Matt held up his hands. "Whoa. Hold it. We're sharing the chores, remember? You don't cook every night. It's every other night. And I'm only supposed to do the dishes every other night. You just haven't been pulling your weight lately."

"Hah!" Jenny's hands were on her hips.

"Hah, yourself," Matt threw back.

"We will not be repressed any longer. The

years of servitude are over! In case you haven't
heard, it's the nineties now. Women are free!" She
threw her arms out dramatically, as if dropping the
weights of chains and shackles.

"I love it when she talks like that," Sly muttered.

"This isn't a feminist issue," Matt pointed
out, walking away from her. "You're just plain lazy,
Jenny. If you don't want to cook and do the dishes,
take it up with Mom and Dad. Hi, guys!" he greeted
Sly and Tony.

Jenny steamed over to them, glaring at her
brother. "Yeah, well, who's always saying, 'Gee,
Mom, sorry. I've got so much homework, I can't do
the dishes tonight. Think Jenny could fill in?'"

"Mom doesn't listen to me."

"That's because she's smart. She's a woman!"

"Right on," Sly pronounced, enjoying the
show. Jenny was really worked up. "You know,
you're beautiful when you're angry."

Jenny advanced on him slowly, her cheeks
flushed, her brown eyes shooting sparks. *Whoops,*
Sly thought. "Actually, Jenny, I agree with you,"
he put in quickly.

"You do?" Matt and Jenny said in unison.

Sly nodded emphatically. "Men need to be
men, and women, well . . . they need to be women."
That wasn't quite what he'd meant to say. "I mean,
we have separate needs because we're different.

Women do one thing and their men take care of them."

"Can it, Winkle!" Jenny flared.

"Just a sec. What I meant to say was that men are the hunters; women are the gatherers. We must work together."

"Do you do the dishes at your house?" Jenny demanded.

"Heck, no," Sly responded instantly. "What do you take me for?"

"You are a macho-jerk, male chauvinist pig of the worst kind!" she yelled at him.

"Yeah, but how do you really feel?" Tony murmured, and then hurried to answer another one of Sharkey's bellows.

"Look, Jenny, you do your part, and I'll do my part, and that's that," Matt said equably.

"Yeah, you do the work, and Matt and I'll go out and have fun," Sly said with a grin. Jenny gasped in fury, and Sly couldn't help adding, "Is that real steam coming out of your ears?"

She sank stiffly into the chair next to him. Well, at least Sly had her full attention now. In fact, she was homed in on him like a heat-seeking missile. Sly felt encouraged.

"The only thing you're good for," she said with a distinct frost, "is being California Dreams' manager, and you seem to have messed that up, too."

11

"You're not going to bring up that Jason Priestley mix-up, are you?"

"That was you who started that rumor?" Matt demanded.

"If someone said I started that rumor, it's a rumor," Sly defended himself.

"I'm talking about the demo tape," Jenny enlightened him.

"The demo tape?"

"Yes, the demo tape. The demo tape that you signed us up to make and then couldn't pay for? Ring any distant bells in that barren landscape up there?" She knocked lightly on his head. "You lost all the money we had gotten together to make that professional tape!"

Matt hid a grin. It was nice to have Jenny's wrath focused on a more deserving guy. And Sly was definitely a more deserving guy.

"Don't smile." Jenny whipped around to stare at him. Matt wiped the grin off his face. "And don't think this means I'm vacuuming for you Friday night!"

"I ended up getting our money back, didn't I?" Sly sputtered. "And I nearly died being Bubba's slave to pay him back for the money I borrowed."

"Borrowed and lost," Jenny reminded him.

"Didn't everything turn out all right?" Sly shot back. "Well, didn't it?"

Jenny didn't immediately answer. Sly gave her a warm look. She was melting. He could tell.

"Too bad a major recording label hasn't shown any interest in the Dreams," Matt added.

Jenny made a face. "That *would* be nice," she agreed, mellowing yet further.

Wheels started turning in Sly's head. Was there one man in this two-bit town able to leap tall buildings in a single bound *and* get California Dreams on the fast track to success?

Why, yes. Sly Winkle was that man. The coolest, most-happening man on this corner of the planet.

Winning Jenny was just a matter of time—and a foolproof plan. With the help of the demo and his cousin Charlie at Coastal Sounds recording studio . . . hey, success was practically in the bag!

Chapter 2

Sly continued to think up a new plan to win Jenny back as Tony finished taking Matt and Jenny's orders. Matt teased Jenny some more about her chores at home, and Jenny made a few more remarks about women's lib.

"Okay, okay." Tony pulled a pencil from behind his ear and did some fast figuring on his notepad. "Two Shark burgers with cheese and two orders of fries."

"Make that one fry," Jenny cut in. "Too much fat."

"As if it would make any difference on your perfect body," Sly said, eyeing her model-slim figure.

Jenny rolled her eyes and chose to ignore him.

"And one chocolate-pineapple shake," Tony finished, shuddering.

"Yech!" Matt looked at Sly as if he'd just climbed out from beneath a rock.

"The immature taste buds of an under-developed species," Jenny declared loftily.

"Hey." Sly pointed to himself. "I'm sitting here."

Tony screwed up his face in serious concentration, his pencil figuring busily. "Two Shark burgers with cheese at two eighty-nine is five seventy-eight for the burgers . . . did you guys want extra pickles with that?"

"No," Jenny and Matt chorused.

"Only ten cents more," Tony added helpfully.

"*No!*" they repeated.

"Okay, okay. Two large fries . . ."

"One!" Jenny yelled.

"Oh, yeah, yeah . . . one large fry at seventy-nine cents. Let's see, there's about fifty-seven fries per order so that's . . . how much per fry?"

"Who cares?" Matt asked.

"Sharkey cares," Sly explained. He brought Jenny and Matt up to date and finished with, "Tony's got to up his customer-money intake or it's the unemployment line."

"That's terrible!" Jenny's mouth dropped in

disbelief. "He can't do that. You're one of the best employees he's got."

"Why, thank you, Jenny." Tony flashed an appreciative grin.

"Well, I mean, you're not bad," she amended, glancing at the other waiters in the room who were bustling to take orders. Tony was the only one talking to his friends. "Actually, now that I think about it, you do need help. Maybe you'd better get back to work."

"What do you think I'm doing? I'm taking an order here!" Tony continued figuring. "We gotta charge more for french fries. Do you realize they're less than a cent apiece?"

Matt shook his head. "Tony, do the words 'You're losing it' have any special meaning here?"

"I've got to keep this job!"

"We know," Jenny soothed. "Maybe you should just check with another customer."

"Yeah? Who?" Tony demanded, gesturing. "All the other customers have already been served."

Sharkey's front door opened with a bang. A rush of sea-tanged air preceded a beautiful girl with long blond hair, who rushed breathlessly into the restaurant. Tiffani Smith, dressed in a hot pink summer top and white denim shorts, greeted her friends with a wide, sweet smile and sparkling eyes.

"Hey, Tiffani," Tony said. "You look hungry.

How about one of Tony Wicks's special, super-duper, you're-dying-for-it, ultimate shakes?"

"I can't eat! I'm too excited. Guess what?" she cried, jumping up and down.

"I'll bite—what?" Sly asked.

"I've met the coolest guy!" She hugged herself with delight. "His name's Drew. Isn't that just the coolest?"

"Well, I'm all a-flutter," Matt said dryly.

"He can sing, play the guitar, and even do backup on drums. I mean, he is great!"

Matt, Jenny, Tony, and Sly all looked at Tiffani. She was known for her enthusiasm, and as backup guitar and vocals for the Dreams, she knew music. But sometimes her enthusiasm ran away with her, and there had been times when it had gotten them all into trouble.

"He sounds fabulous," Jenny agreed.

"He wants to be in the band. Now, I know—"

"Be in the band?" Matt interrupted. "Tiffani, the Dreams have been a group for a long time. We're set. Jenny's keyboards, I'm lead guitar, you're backup guitar, and Tony's drums. We all do the vocals. We don't need anybody else."

"And I'm the manager," Sly reminded them all, though no one seemed to pay particular attention to him.

Tiffani went on, "But I thought, you know, if one of us got sick or something and we had a big gig

. . . maybe we could use Drew. I know you're all going to love him!"

She glanced pleadingly from one face to another. It was so hard to say no to her. Tiffani was as sweet as honey and as innocent as a baby.

"Look, we're really not in the market for another band member, but why don't you bring him to our next rehearsal and we'll listen to him," Matt suggested.

"Oh, thanks! You're the greatest." Tiffani hugged him. "I know this is going to work out. I can just feel it."

"Wicks!" Sharkey bellowed from the kitchen.

"Sure you don't want that shake, Tiff?"

She shook her blond locks, and with a sigh, Tony made a fast exit.

"Sharkey wouldn't really fire him, would he?" Jenny asked.

"Nah." Sly shook his head.

"He's all talk," Matt agreed.

"Why would Sharkey fire Tony?" Tiffani asked, concerned.

"Long story," was Matt's answer.

All four of them looked at each other. Tony lived with his dad, who was a teacher at Pacific Coast High, and Tony needed the extra money his job at Sharkey's provided to buy some of the extras outside the family budget. Besides, for all his complaining, Tony really *liked* working at Sharkey's.

"We've got to help him," Matt said, verbalizing the thought in each of their minds.

"How?" Jenny asked.

"Leave it to me," Sly informed them all. Matt and Jenny exchanged looks, and Tiffani glanced anxiously at Sly. "I mean it," Sly persisted. "I'll make sure everything works out."

"Why am I worried?" Jenny asked, arching one brow.

Sly smiled at her. The more he thought about it, the more he was convinced that his earlier plan was the answer for all of them. All he had to do was get California Dreams hooked up with a recording label; then the jobs and money would come flying in. Tony wouldn't have to work at Sharkey's, even though he actually seemed to like the place. The Dreams would be on their way to glory, and he would have Jennifer Garrison in his strong, male arms. All he had to do was check in with Cousin Charlie, who'd helped them get the demo tape in the first place, and wham-o! Success, fortune, and fame were awaiting all of them.

"Trust me," Sly said, smoothing back his hair with one hand.

Jenny smiled faintly. "Sly, those two words on your lips send chills down my back."

"My lips are good for more than talk. . . ." He leaned closer.

She pushed him away. "Too bad your chocolate-pineapple shake isn't here yet. I think I've found a perfect place for it." With that, she pointed to his head, laughing mischievously.

Yep, Sly realized. *She's definitely melting for me.*

Two days later, the Dreams assembled in the Garrisons' garage, their normal rehearsal spot. Matt fiddled on the corner piano, picking out a song. There were some pieces of music floating through his mind, and it just took time to get them down in logical order. He glanced around.

Tony was flipping his drumsticks into space and catching them behind his back. Sly was looking into the chip of broken mirror hanging on the wall, admiring his reflection. Jenny was staring off into space.

They were all waiting for Tiffani to arrive.

"She's generally on time," Jenny said aloud.

They all grunted in acknowledgment.

Matt turned back to the piano, and Jenny came over and glanced down at the bits and pieces of music Matt had jotted onto some blank pages. She hummed the melody, liking what she was hearing. Matt had a knack for songwriting. California Dreams' best songs were the ones he'd developed when he'd been working through some deep personal feelings of his own.

Personal feelings . . .

Jenny sighed. She'd suffered a few personal feelings of her own lately. It hadn't been that long since she'd been with Sean, her ex-boyfriend. She'd really thought they had something special, but it had ended when he'd moved away. Of course, they'd told each other they'd write, and for a few weeks they had. But then they had kind of drifted apart. Sean's letters and phone calls had gradually lessened and then stopped altogether. He hadn't written to her in a long while, and she hadn't felt the urge to write, either.

She knew, as he probably did, that it was over.

What's wrong with me? Jenny asked herself now. *Why does it seem like the only guy who likes me is Sly?*

She glanced his way. When she was feeling generous, she had to admit Sly was good-looking, in a slimy sort of way. Dark hair, slick clothes, cute smile.

He glanced her way and caught her staring. Lifting one brow, he sent her a slow wink.

Jenny inwardly groaned. Too bad he was so obnoxious!

The door rattled open and slammed against the wall. Tiffani bounced in.

"About time," Tony grumbled, and then stopped cold as he—and all the rest of the Dreams—got their first look at Tiffani's new friend Drew, who strolled in behind her.

Wow! Jenny thought, her gaze dropping slowly over Drew's muscled, six-foot-three-inch frame before sliding back up again. His hair was blond and shoulder length. His biceps bulged. His chest was wide, wide, wide! He looked like he belonged in an action/adventure flick.

And then he smiled slowly, an infectious grin guaranteed to melt the most fervent skeptic's heart.

No way, Jenny reminded herself, refusing to be fooled. Someone who looked that good was undoubtedly misfiring in the brain department. She'd seen her share of muscle-bound Neanderthals, and to a one, they'd all spent more time exercising their bods than using their brains.

She glanced at Tiffani's shining face. Too bad. It looked as if Tiff really liked the guy.

"This is Drew!" Tiffani bubbled.

Drew held out a huge paw to Sly, who was the closest. "Nice to meet you. Gosh, I'm glad to be here."

"The pleasure's all yours," Sly said, wincing as Drew squeezed his hand.

Matt came over and Drew shook hands with him. A spasm crossed Matt's face. He stared down at his hand when Drew finally released it. "I may never play again," he mumbled.

"Yo," Tony said, lifting his palm in a high five. Drew slapped it so hard Tony fell back a step. "Major power there, man," Tony murmured as he

22

joined Matt and Sly. They all looked at each other, and Jenny could see that their eagerness to include Drew was at a new, all-time low.

"Well?" Jenny said, indicating Matt's guitar. "Let's see what you've got . . . Drew."

"This is fabulous, guys!" Tiffani blushed, snuggling up next to Drew. He dropped an enormous arm around her in a protective hug.

Like being squeezed by an orangutan, Jenny thought darkly.

Drew picked up Matt's guitar, familiarized himself with it, and then glanced up expectantly. "What should I play?"

"Whatever you want." Matt shrugged. "Just jump in and show us your stuff."

"Should I sing, too?"

"Give us all you've got," Matt suggested. The three boys gave each other silent looks that revealed their negative feelings about the whole situation.

Jenny crossed the room to join them, lifting her brows. Tiffani stayed close to Drew, but she kept darting looks over her shoulder at her friends and smiling brightly.

"She really wants him in the band," Jenny whispered.

"Bad idea," Sly muttered.

Matt sighed. "I just hate to hurt Tiffani's feelings."

23

"Maybe he'll be a radical bust," Tony remarked hopefully.

"What if he's not?" Jenny worried aloud.

"Shhh . . ." Matt shushed them as Drew began picking out the notes to one of Matt's songs. He'd clearly been practicing, and there was no doubt that Tiffani had given him a copy of the music. Pretty soon, he added his voice, which was higher than Matt's but right on key. It didn't quite have Matt's resonance, however, but it was okay.

In spite of herself, Jenny found herself nodding to the music. Drew was playing one of Matt's catchier tunes, and though he didn't possess Matt's musical timing and skill, he wasn't horrible. Still, Drew wasn't really Dreams material. She just hoped Tiffani would realize that.

" . . . it's our time, baby!" Drew cried in a high falsetto, finishing the song with a wild gliss on his guitar and an energetic leap in the air. He dropped to one knee and then strummed the last notes madly, throwing an arm skyward and bowing.

"Nice finish," Sly muttered sarcastically.

"That was great!" Tiffani clapped enthusiastically and ran over to her friends. "Well?" she whispered.

"Not bad . . . ," Matt struggled.

"There's some—potential—there," Jenny agreed, forcing a smile.

"He looks good," Toni pointed out.

Tiffani beamed. "You really think so? I do, too!" She raced back to Drew, who twirled her around in a bear hug.

"We gotta send Drew back to the beach, pronto," Sly remarked flatly.

"I agree." Tony nodded.

"So do I. But how do we tell Tiff?" Matt asked.

"I'll do it," Jenny said on a sigh. "She'll understand, I think. . . ."

Jenny glanced over at Tiffani and Drew. They were staring into each other's eyes as if they were the only two people on the planet.

"But I'll do it later," she added, and Matt, Tony, and Sly all grinned knowingly. "I really will!" she insisted.

"Better do it before Drew starts thinking this is his home," Tony pointed out.

Jenny stole another glance at Tiffani and Drew, fighting a tiny flame of jealousy inside her at the obvious affection between them. *When am I going to find the right guy?* she thought sadly to herself.

Chapter 3

Sly rubbed his hands together as he stood in the hallway of Coastal Sounds, the recording studio where his cousin Charlie worked. Charlie had been the one who'd helped produce California Dreams' demo tape, the tape meant to propel the Dreams into the "big time." Unfortunately, things hadn't quite worked out the way they'd all hoped.

Sly had had some serious trouble getting the money together as promised, and that had kind of put good ol' Charlie in the hot seat for a while. But, hey, everything worked out in the end. The Dreams had gotten the demo and Charlie had kept his job.

"No reason for him to still be mad at me," Sly remarked aloud as he paced the hallway, waiting for Charlie to appear. "No reason at all."

Footsteps sounded at the end of the hall. Sly

looked up. Charlie, accompanied by a young, brown-haired woman in a skintight black dress, had finally gotten the message that someone was waiting for him.

"Hey, Charles, my man!" Sly lifted a hand in greeting.

The expectant look on Charlie's face turned to disbelief, then annoyance. "What are *you* doing here?"

"Is that any way to greet your favorite cousin?" Sly flashed the girl a grin. "Hi, gorgeous. Sly Winkle." He extended his hand, which she recoiled from as if it were covered with slime.

"Later," she said to Charlie.

"What's her problem?" Sly asked.

"You! I told her what you did." Charlie pushed open the door to the control room above the main recording studio.

"Wait a minute here," Sly protested, sliding his foot inside just before Charlie slammed the door. "Ouch! That hurt! If I didn't know the depth of our familial bond, I might take offense."

"*Take* offense," Charlie encouraged. "It was meant to be offensive."

"You're not still torked about that little misunderstanding over the demo tape, are you?"

"Sly, what do you want? Say it, listen hard while I turn you down, and then *get out*."

Sly frowned. This wasn't going quite as well as

he'd hoped. But it was a minor snag in the overall plan to win Jenny's heart along with the band's enduring gratitude. "All I need is some advice . . . and maybe a good word or two placed with the right people."

"No."

"You see"—Sly held up his hands, painting a broad picture for Charlie to envision—"California Dreams has a great tape, but it's not getting any airtime. The band needs a push. In fact, we need a recording label behind us. Something big like Atlantic Records or EMI."

Charlie doubled over in a choking fit of laughter.

"You don't think the Dreams are good enough?" Sly demanded.

"Those labels are primo! You need connections to get heard. Real connections. Besides, I thought you sent the demo to every label around."

"I did," Sly jumped in, giving him a what-do-you-take-me-for? look.

"Man, it's hard to break in. And unless you're talking smaller potatoes, don't look to me for help."

This was the opening Sly had been waiting for. "What about BBG Records?"

"BBG Records!" Charlie whooped with laughter. "You've got to be kidding!"

Sly winced inwardly. BBG stood for Brad Bartley Griffen, Jr., the owner of BBG Records, but because the record label was known for its less than well-known groups—groups like Tinker and the Bells—it didn't get much respect.

"If I remember correctly, you said that you know Brad Bartley Griffen, Jr.," Sly reminded his cousin.

"BBG himself," Charlie agreed. "A real charmer."

"He's successful. Look what he did for BBG Records."

Before Brad Bartley Griffen, Jr., had taken over Omni Records and changed its name, it had been an easy-listening label headed straight downhill to nowheres-ville. But with BBG, Jr.'s expertise, BBG Records now produced demos and CDs instead of vinyl. Though Sly had purposely stayed away from the label because it was a bit of a small fry in the recording biz, he now saw its potential.

"They've had some major hits," Sly defended the label.

Charlie stopped laughing long enough to stare hard at Sly. "You're serious!"

"California Dreams needs airtime. I bet BBG can give it to us."

"Well . . . well . . . I think you're right," Charlie suddenly agreed. "In fact, the more I think about it, BBG's perfect for you. Stay right there. I'll call him myself and set up a time for you two to meet."

"Great." Charlie's sudden about-face sent off warning bells in Sly's mind, but the bells were silenced when he envisioned Jenny's expressive eyes gazing deeply into his, her arms sliding around his neck, her luscious pink lips moving toward his.

"BBG. Yeah." Sly rubbed his hands together again. "This is going to be perfect. Just perfect."

"Hey, how's it going, Tiff?" Jenny asked brightly as she stopped by Tiffani's house after school. Lately, Tiffani had been kind of hard to find alone. She was always with Drew.

"I am so glad you stopped by," Tiffani greeted her. "We've got to go shopping. I've worn the same bathing suit three times when Drew and I have been together. I've got to get a new one."

"Okay." Jenny nodded. "I wanted to talk about Drew, anyway."

"My favorite subject! Come on. Let's head to the mall."

During the entire drive, Tiffani chattered on about Drew as if he were God's gift to the female population as a whole and to Tiffani specifically. Knowing she had to tell Tiffani that Drew wasn't welcome in the band, Jenny sank lower and lower in the passenger seat of Tiffani's stepmother's car. She felt like a heel, especially since Drew wasn't a bad guy. He seemed to really like Tiffani, and Jenny hated being the bearer of bad news.

"I should have given this job to Sly. It's the kind of thing he feeds on," Jenny muttered beneath her breath.

"What's that about Sly?" Tiffani asked as she pulled into a parking spot near the main entrance to the mall.

Jenny shook her head in disbelief. "How do you do it? Every time we go somewhere, you find a parking place right in front."

"Positive thinking," Tiffani said cheerily. "Think good thoughts and good things happen!"

Jenny sank still lower.

Fifteen minutes later, Jenny was pacing outside the dressing room of Suits Me, their favorite bathing suit shop. Tiffani had discarded one pink string bikini and was currently trying on an aqua-and-gold Hawaiian-print one that covered a few more millimeters of skin.

Jenny practiced telling Tiffani the truth in front of one of the store's mirrors.

"Although Drew's a great guy, a really, really nice, good-looking hunk of man . . . no!" She sucked in a frustrated breath, scowled at her reflection, and started again. "Tiffani, Drew sounded terrific at the rehearsal, but the Dreams don't need him. He's just extra baggage."

She groaned and lifted her arms over her head, easing tension from her shoulders. Taking a deep breath, she forced a smile until the image staring back at her from the mirror looked happier and more at ease.

"Tiffani," she tried again. "I think Drew is a really great guy. I don't know him very well, but he's a . . . a babe!" She laughed aloud. Good grief! She sounded like Sly. "He's cute—and those muscles and that smile! But, Tiffani, he's not right for California Dreams. I mean, we just don't need him."

She stepped back from the mirror, thinking over her words. They weren't half-bad. And they were true. Drew seemed like a really great guy. And he was uncomplicated in a refreshing way. She was tired of guys who always had an angle. It was one thing to be a feminist and want a guy with a brain, but it was also nice to be with someone you could just relax with.

Confused, Jenny considered what that meant. Could she, razor-witted, ambitious, driven Jennifer Garrison, actually fall for a guy like Drew?

Impossible!

Yet . . .

For a moment, she closed her eyes and let herself recall Drew's charming smile and his rumpled, thick blond hair. She imagined what it would feel like to be in his arms. Protected. Safe. Loved.

A hot wave of jealousy enveloped her.

Her eyes flew open, and she stared at her reflection in shock.

"Oh, no," she whispered, hating herself a little.

She had a crush on her best friend's guy!

That night at dinner, Matt stared across the table at Jenny. She looked a little pale, but more disturbing than that, she'd hardly said two words all night! Something was seriously wrong. Jenny always had a lot to say about everything.

"You're on dish detail tonight, Matt," his mother reminded him as she cleared the table. "And, Jenny, you have a date with the vacuum cleaner."

"Uh-huh," Jenny murmured distractedly, gazing off into space.

Their little brother, Dennis, looked up at her, shrugged, and asked Matt, "Is she in love again?"

That was it! Matt recognized the signs, too, now that Dennis had pointed them out: starry eyes; distracted attention; loss of appetite.

Except Jenny looked absolutely miserable.

"Who's the guy, Jen?" Matt asked when they were alone. Jenny was still sitting at the table, as if planted there for the next millennium.

"Huh?" She turned to look at him, but her dark eyes weren't focused.

Matt waved a hand in front of her face. "Come back! Come back!" He gazed imploringly at the ceiling. "Whoever took Jenny and left this alien in her place, please bring her back. She's a royal pain in the neck, but we need her for the band!"

"Stop!" Jenny swatted at him, annoyed.

"What's going on with you?"

"Nothing! Do you have to be so nosy?"

"It's a new guy, isn't it?"

"No!" Jenny yelled a little too emphatically.

Matt lifted one brow. "You haven't been seeing anyone lately. Unless it's Tony or Sly. . . ."

"Please! Sly! Don't make me throw up."

Baffled, Matt frowned. He'd never seen Jenny so touchy. Normally, she raved about the latest love of her life to anyone and everyone within a ten-mile radius.

Deciding it was time to shift gears, he asked, "Did you talk to Tiffani about Drew?" The look that crossed Jenny's face was indescribable. With a lightning bolt of insight, Matt suddenly understood. "Oh, no," he groaned.

"What?" Jenny regarded him suspiciously.

"It's Drew!"

"No!"

"Yes, it is! You've fallen for Tiffani's Drew!"

"I have not!" she screeched, leaping from her chair and standing in front of him, fists clenched.

Matt started to laugh. He couldn't help himself. Jenny was always so in control that it was *funny* to see her so unraveled.

"If you keep laughing I'll . . . I'll . . .," she sputtered, infuriated.

"I know what you'll do. You'll do the vacuuming *and* the dishes, or I'll tell Drew how you feel!"

"That's blackmail!" Jenny gasped.

Matt grinned. "Okay, listen. I'll make a deal with you. I won't tell a soul, but you've got my chores for a month."

"No way! I won't! I'll—"

"In exchange for that," Matt overrode her, "*I'll* tell Tiffani that Drew is out of the band, since I get the feeling you never got that far."

All the starch went out of Jenny at once. Defeated, she sank back into a chair. "No, I didn't," she admitted.

"Do I have to do everything for you?" he teased.

"Matt . . . ," Jenny started, and then cut herself off.

He waited for a few moments, realized how much she was struggling with herself, and finally came to the rescue. "I know you'd never intentionally hurt Tiffani, but sometimes it's hard to hide your feelings."

"I don't think I even really like him, Matt."

"Well, there's something going on, isn't there?"

She sighed and nodded. "He just seems like

35

a really great guy, and I wish I had someone like him."

Matt frowned. "Be careful, okay?"

Jenny nodded, glad Matt understood.

He glanced at his watch. "And get to work. The dishes are calling."

With that, he grabbed his coat and headed out the door.

Chapter 4

"I've got it all figured out," Tony said to Sly as he was throwing on his Sharkey's uniform. Since Tony had a shift and Sly was starving, the two boys had come to the restaurant straight from school. "All I have to do is serve my friends and the Sharkman'll be rolling in the dough! I've got lots of friends. So anybody else who walks in the door is gravy, man."

"Wicks."

Sharkey's voice at his elbow made Tony jump half a foot. "Whoa, there, Shark. You kind of took me by surprise."

"Your theory's all wet. Since your friends don't pay," he pointed out, pushing his face in front of Tony's, "I'm losing money on 'em."

"They pay! Don't they, Sly?"

Sharkey turned accusing eyes on Sly. Sly smiled sickly, remembering all the free meals he'd wangled from Sharkey himself. "Every time I've had a freebie, the Dreams have played as payment," Sly reminded Sharkey.

"Like I hired 'em or something!" Sharkey snorted.

"Jenny and Matt and Tiffani have paid lots of times," Tony defended himself.

"Yeah? Well, they don't come in every day, and when they do, they don't always order. They just sit around and yak, yak, yak. Sometimes they share. Sometimes they just get drinks. Factor that into your equation, Wicks," he snapped out as he stalked away. "And get to work!"

"You sure showed him," Sly said.

"Man, how can I increase my dollars per serving? I need a serious in-flow of currency here. When I think of how I'm supposed to figure this out, my brain cells start smoking!" Tony thought that one over. "It hurts to be smart."

"Tell me about it," Sly muttered, checking Sharkey's fish-shaped clock on the wall. "Gotta go."

"Where're you going?"

"I've got a meeting," Sly answered mysteriously. "One that could solve your money problems and change California Dreams' destiny forever!"

● ● ●

Matt's gaze had followed Jenny around the house all morning. Now she was on her knees, dusting the coffee table in the living room. Guilt gnawed at him. She was working pretty hard and even though she'd really been a pain in the neck by slacking off before, now she was making up for it in spades. Matt knew Jenny didn't want to face Tiffani and Drew, but the depth of her desire to steer clear of them bothered Matt. Maybe she liked Drew more than she'd admitted, which could mean real problems for Tiffani and Jenny's friendship, not to mention what it could do to California Dreams.

And the Dreams had just gotten back on track! The band had suffered through some tough times when Jenny had fallen for a guy from a different group, Solar Energy, and had started singing with them. For a while, it had looked like the Dreams were history. Matt had even tried filling Jenny's empty slot with his on-again-off-again girlfriend, Randi Jo, but that hadn't worked—which was just as well, since he and Randi Jo were currently off again.

But then Jenny had come back, and the Dreams had jumped back on track. Now just when everything seemed to be running smoothly, this thing with Drew had cropped up.

"Drew," Matt muttered, shaking his head.

Jenny looked up. "Did you say something?"

"Not really."

"Have you talked to Tiffani and Drew yet?" she asked.

"Tiffani's supposed to be bringing Drew by soon."

"Here?" She leaped to her feet, yanking the scarf from around her hair.

"It isn't a fashion contest. I have to give them the news about Drew, so I asked Tiffani to bring him along. Might as well give it to him straight," he finished grimly.

Jenny raced to the mirror, fluffed at her hair, made desperate gagging noises in her throat, and ran for her room. Matt shook his head as the kitchen doorbell rang and Tiffani ducked her head inside.

"Anybody home?" she called.

"Right here," Matt said.

Drew came in with Tiffani. They were holding hands, and Tiffani was bursting with excitement. "Well?" she asked, her smile wide with expectation.

"Drew, you sounded really great. I mean it." Matt mentally crossed his fingers.

Tiffani bounced on her feet. "I knew it! I knew it! Oh, Matt, you're terrific!"

"No, wait, I—"

"This is the best, man," Drew said, nodding. "The best."

"Give me a chance to finish."

"Hi, guys," Jenny greeted them from the

stairway. She took the last few steps in a slow saunter, and then walked to the stove, picked up the teapot, and poured herself a cup, smiling at Tiffani and Drew over the rim.

Matt's jaw dropped. She'd changed into a white shirt and black vest that sported a wild grouping of antique silver buttons. Her hair was perfect. Trouble. Big, *big* trouble.

"Hi, Jenny. Great vest," Tiffani enthused. "Where'd you get it?"

"Vests R Us," she said. Drew laughed and she laughed back. "Just kidding. I got it at The Jeanery."

Tiffani's smooth brow pulled into a frown as Jenny and Drew shared "a moment."

Matt had to do something fast. "Look, I'm sorry. We really don't have room for Drew in the band." He turned to the blond muscleman. "Your style's a little different from ours. We've kind of got our sound down, and though we liked what we heard, it just isn't right for us."

A moment of pure silence followed. Matt held his breath. Drew looked from Jenny to Tiffani, whose lips were parted in dismay.

"That's okay, man," he said. "I was just glad to have the chance."

Jenny's breath rushed out. "You really were good."

"Thanks." He grinned and shrugged in embarrassment.

41

"You're not upset?" Tiffani asked.

"Nah."

"You can jam with us anytime," Matt offered.

Drew shook Matt's hand. Then he turned to Jenny for a second, seemed about to say something, and then clasped Tiffani's hand again and said, "I'll be back," in a passable Arnold Schwarzenneger imitation as he guided Tiffani toward the door.

"See you guys at the street dance?" Jenny called anxiously.

"Yeah . . . sure . . ." Drew's voice drifted back to her.

Jenny's gaze clung to the door long after he and Tiffani had left. "He's really cool."

"Hmmm . . ."

"What do you mean by that?" Jenny asked him.

Matt didn't answer. The jury was still out on Drew as far as he was concerned. Time would tell if the guy was as great as Jenny and Tiffani seemed to think he was.

Brad Bartley Griffen, Jr.'s recording studio was a plain gray building with flashy neon lights surrounding an arched entryway that reminded Sly of one of those old Wurlitzer jukeboxes. Pink, blue, green, and yellow neon strips glowed and buzzed overhead as he entered the first-floor foyer.

A vacant-eyed receptionist regarded him without interest.

"I'm here to see Mr. Griffen," Sly said, straightening his lapels. He'd worn his coolest clothes: a fluorescent orange T-shirt beneath an iridescent indigo jacket.

"BBG's busy all day. Leave a message."

"I have an appointment," Sly informed her.

Her look said, "Oh, really?"

"Really," Sly answered, leaning a hip on her polished black marble desktop. "Why don't you check with the boss? Tell him Sly's here."

Heaving a sigh, she punched several buttons and announced in a bored tone, "Somebody named Slick here to see BBG."

"Sly!"

"Sly," she repeated into the receiver with a curl of her lip. A moment later, one pencil-thin eyebrow quirked in surprise.

Hah! Sly thought. *Gotcha!*

"The elevator's over there. Third floor. Double doors at the end of the hall." She pointed with ill grace and turned back to opening envelopes with one long, wicked-looking red nail.

Sly patted his pocket to make sure the demo tape was inside and practiced his delivery on the ride up the elevator. He had to come in like a tornado and sweep BBG off his feet. A little razzle-dazzle, the demo tape, and *bam!* History would be made, and he'd have BBG eating out of the palm of his hand!

The elevator bell dinged politely, and the doors slid open. Sly stepped into a hallway covered with lush steel-gray carpet and mahogany-paneled walls. He inhaled deeply.

"Ah, the smell of money and success!"

Whistling, he strolled to the double doors at the end of the hall and knocked loudly.

"Come in!" a voice yelled.

Sly pushed open one of the doors. A young man sat at an enormous polished black desk. The phone was glued to his ear and he was talking fast.

"He's perfect. Absolutely perfect. Get him a song in his range and make sure those sideburns grow in. Brooding. That's the look." A pause. "Yeah, sure. Get back to me."

He slammed down the receiver and stared at Sly. Sly stared right back. This was BBG? The guy wasn't much older than he was!

"Refresh my memory," BBG ordered, pushing back his chair. His clothes reeked of money. Just like the whole place. "You are?"

"I'm Sl-Sly Winkle," Sly stammered.

BBG smoothed a hair into place and looked thoughtful. His dark gray suit was more conservative than Sly's outfit was. His shirt was black silk

and he wore maroon suspenders that peeked
out when he thrust his hands into his pockets.
Like now.

BBG got up and walked over to Sly. His black
hair was slicked down. His eyes were narrow and
dark. He sized Sly up with a long, long look.

All of a sudden, he smiled and thrust out his
hand. "Glad to meet you, son. Charlie says you've
got a tape I've got to hear."

Sly shook hands, slightly dazed. Son? Who
was he kidding? "I've got it right here." He plucked
the demo from his pocket and handed it to BBG.

"Hmmm." BBG read the label on the tape.
"California Dreams? Not bad. A little cute, but I
can live with it."

A little cute? Sly thought as BBG pressed a
button on the side of his desk and a section of the
mahogany-paneled wall slid noiselessly back. Who
was he kidding? BBG Records currently was pro-
ducing both Tinker and the Bells and The Breathsprays. A little *cute?*

Behind the wall was a music system to die for.
Sly gaped at all the lights, buttons, and gleaming
black amps, cassette recorders, CD players, and
more. Overhead, recessed lighting illuminated the
vista of electronic equipment as if it were a collec-
tion of priceless art.

BBG slid the tape into place, pressed a button,

and stepped back. Matt's strong voice suddenly poured from the walls and ceiling in a wave of vivid sound. Sly jumped in surprise.

"Wow!" He hadn't noticed the cleverly hidden speaker holes in the geometric slashes of wallpaper.

His voice went unheard beneath Matt's lyrics. BBG listened intently and then fast-forwarded to another section of "Cross My Heart." Jenny's rich voice came next, plaintive in the misery of her song about lost love. After a few moments, he pressed the fast-forward button again until he heard Tiffani's bright, chiming tones blend with Jenny's.

All in all, he listened for less than a minute before snapping the tape out of the player and examining it thoughtfully, as if he could make a decision by the look of it alone.

"Well?" Sly asked, unable to handle the suspense.

"I don't make snap decisions, Mr. Sly." BBG gave a belly laugh.

"Mr. Winkle. But, please, call me by my first name, Sly."

"And I don't make false promises, but . . ." He strode back to his desk, tossed the tape down, and slid Sly a calculated grin. "I like it. I really like it. And when I like something, things happen. Look at this!" He yanked open a drawer and pulled out a plastic CD holder, unsnapped it, and unfolded a piece of paper that had been tucked in with the compact disc.

Sly saw that the paper was a folded poster of Tinker, lead singer for Tinker and the Bells. He was snarling at the camera, which seemed kind of strange since he looked about thirteen.

"Check out this poster!" BBG ordered. "Is that something, or what? Tinker and the Bells were strictly small-time until we did some tinkering of our own." He laughed heartily and slapped Sly on the back. "It's all in the marketing!"

Sly forced a laugh. Boy, was this guy oily! He made the Exxon/Valdez slick seem like a cup of spilled motor fluid.

"Two top-ten songs in the last six months," BBG chortled. "Proper marketing. That's what it takes."

"Absolutely," Sly agreed. "Of course they have to be able to sing, too. And have some musical talent."

"Yeah, right." BBG shrugged. "But image, my man. *Image!*" He yelled so loudly that Sly winced. "Tinker's got the look. Right?"

"The look," Sly agreed vaguely. Actually, Tinker resembled an overgrown elf, dressed in green tights and green eye makeup, which, Sly guessed, was the point. Small-time, he reminded himself, thinking of BBG's reputation. Maybe he ought to grab the demo and book outta there.

BBG snapped his fingers. "That's what sells. The right video, the right costuming."

"And the right sound," Sly added. "Right?"

"Oh, of course. Now, Mr. Sly . . ." BBG put his arm around Sly's shoulders and walked him toward the door. "I don't take on just any group, you understand. They've got to have that something that makes them special."

"Uh-huh."

"I mean, look at Tinker. Is he a sensation, or what?"

"Nice legs," Sly admitted. "Perfect for tights."

"Exactly!" BBG clapped him on the back again and beamed, clearly excited by Sly's grasp of the music industry.

"I think the Dreams have got what it takes. Our lead singer, Matt, is also the group's songwriter. He—"

"Yeah, yeah. We'll talk later. But you and I have an understanding." He looked Sly in the eye. "If I like 'em. And I'm not saying I do, but if I do. You're the one who's going to deliver them."

"Well, of course. No problem. I'm the manager."

"If something falls through, I'm holding you personally responsible."

"Naturally." Sly's smile felt a bit tight.

"Naturally." BBG shook his hand and winked at him.

Sly left with the sinking feeling that he'd just been had. Why did BBG make it sound like talking the Dreams into this would be a problem? If Sly could swing this deal, the Dreams, and Jenny in particular, would be eternally grateful to him.

There was nothing to worry about. He'd break the good news tonight. At the street dance. But first, a quick trip to Sharkey's for a pre-congratulatory Shark burger and chocolate-pineapple shake.

Chapter 5

"What a crowd," Matt said, driving around and around the surrounding blocks, searching for a place to park for the street dance. The deep thrum of bass guitar could be felt like a heartbeat.

"They sound great," Jenny said, making a little face. Solar Energy was playing tonight, and it was the first time she'd seen them perform since her ex-boyfriend, and one-time lead singer for the band, had moved away.

"Who's singing lead now that Sean's gone?" Tiffani asked.

Jenny glanced back as Matt maneuvered into a tight spot. Tiffani and Drew were snuggled together in the backseat like two lovebugs. When Tiffani had asked if she and Drew could ride with

Matt and Jenny, Jenny hadn't known what to say. She'd expected to meet them at the dance, but because of her crush on Drew, she hadn't really wanted to be with them the whole time. It seemed safer to have some distance.

Consequently, she'd fumbled around and made excuses and finally said that she would have to ask Matt, since he was driving. But when she'd approached Matt with her problem, he'd been perfectly obnoxious!

"You've got to get over this infatuation," he'd told her flat out.

Jenny had been incensed. "Infatuation!"

"Tiffani's your best buddy," Matt had pointed out. "You don't even really like Drew. He's not your kind of guy!"

"Who says?"

"I says. Look, I know you've been down since Sean left. Hey, it hasn't been a picnic since Randi Jo and I split up, but that doesn't mean you can poach on Tiffani's guy."

Jenny had wanted to clap her hands over her ears. "I'm not poaching. I just think it's nice that he's so—nice."

"Wait! Let me write that down. What great lyrics: It's nice that he's so nice."

"Oh, cut it out!"

She'd thrown a sofa pillow at him, annoyed, and things had deteriorated rapidly from there.

Matt had grabbed another pillow and bopped her on the head. Half angry, half laughing, she'd started slamming him with another one, and then they'd whacked and hit each other until they were both breathless from laughing.

That's when their mother had arrived and noticed the ripping seams of one of her sofa throw pillows. Jenny had spent the rest of the afternoon fighting the sewing machine, which stubbornly refused to work, breaking needle upon needle, while she repaired the damage. In a fit of frustration, she'd finally thrown herself on the floor and howled, "It's not fair!" which had gained her no sympathy at all.

In the end, she'd called Tiffani and invited her and Drew to go with them. Then she'd spent an hour on her hair and clothes. Her bedroom had ended up looking as though a cyclone had swept through it, but her furious attempts to make herself beautiful hadn't helped. She didn't feel right about her appearance. Part of her hair stuck up and wouldn't lie down, no matter what she did. Her jeans and denim top seemed drab next to Tiffani's bright colors.

And, worst of all, the entire fuss was because she had a thing for *Tiffani*'s guy!

Jenny groaned inwardly. She ought to be drawn and quartered for thinking such thoughts.

"I don't think they've replaced Sean," Matt

answered Tiffani as he cut the engine. "Some of the other band members are filling in."

"They do sound cool," Drew admitted.

They all climbed out of the car and were greeted by a swell of music. Threading their way through the mass of bobbing people, they crowded together near one side of the bandstand. The street was blocked off on both ends, and Solar Energy stood on a raised platform that was surrounded by twinkling white lights. A mob of kids were dancing in the street, and the whole periphery was a wall of moving people. At the far end stood a row of booths that sold twisty fries, sodas, snow cones, and hot dogs.

"Want to get something to eat?" Tiffani asked Drew.

"I do," Matt spoke up.

"Why don't you go with Matt?" Drew suggested to Tiffani. "I'll stay with Jenny until you get back."

Tiffani looked astonished. "Okay. What do you want?"

"Surprise me."

"Jenny?" Matt asked, his gaze meaningful.

She glared at him. What did he think she was going to do? Steal Drew away from Tiffani while they made a run for twisty fries? "Surprise me," she muttered through her teeth.

Her nerves were on edge. She and Drew stood

side by side, neither saying anything as they listened to the band. Solar Energy was good, but without Sean, it just didn't seem the same.

"Sorry we couldn't use you for the Dreams," Jenny apologized.

"Ah, no problem. You really work together as a team. I understand."

"That's very—mature of you!" Jenny laughed.

Drew smiled, and Jenny's heart melted a little. *Put a lid on it,* she reminded herself quickly.

"So, you used to date a guy from this band?" Drew asked, jerking his head to indicate Solar Energy. At her look of surprise, he revealed, "Tiffani told me. She said he moved to San Francisco and that you're really bummed."

"Yep." *Thanks, Tiffani,* she thought darkly, and then was ashamed of herself.

"Do you guys still talk?"

For a moment, Jenny thought he meant her and Tiffani, and her blood froze. Then she realized he meant Sean. *You idiot!* she berated herself. "We did for a while, but it got kind of weird. I wrote some letters, but I didn't have much to say."

"Yeah." He nodded sagely.

"I guess, if you really want a relationship to work, it needs to be geographically desirable."

"Huh?" He gazed at her, his green eyes dark

and mysterious. Jenny was momentarily mesmerized.

"I said," she shouted above the noise, "a relationship has to be geographically desirable. You know, you have to live near each other."

"Oh . . . yeah. Hey, Jenny, you want to dance?"

"Well, sure . . ."

He grabbed her arm and guided her through the throng to a spot in the center where the full sound of the band could be heard. Just when he pulled her into his arms, Tiffani and Matt appeared.

"Drew!" Tiffani said in surprise.

"Jenny!" Matt echoed.

Jenny's heart sank. She pasted on a smile for Matt and accepted the soda he thrust into her hands.

"We thought we'd cut through this mob," Tiffani explained, "but maybe it wasn't such a good idea."

"Let's find a spot on the sidelines," Drew suggested.

Jenny sighed. Their dance, at least for the moment, was over. Maybe that was for the best. A few minutes later, Drew pulled Tiffani to the center of the street and they swayed gently to a love song.

"Solar Energy's not the same," Matt mumbled around a mouthful of fries.

"You're probably glad, aren't you?" Jenny snapped. "You were really jealous of them."

"Hey, I got over it, didn't I?"

"Only after acting like a real jerk!"

Matt stared at her. "What's your problem?"

"You! You're acting like my keeper!"

"Oh, I get it." Matt shot a sideways look toward Tiffani and Drew. "It's all my fault that you've got a major thing for your best friend's guy."

Jenny steamed. She just hated it when he was right.

"He doesn't seem to be too upset that we couldn't use him," Matt mused. "Amazing."

"Why? Because he took the news like a man?"

"Ooooh." Matt started laughing, which only infuriated Jenny more because she knew she sounded like an idiot.

At that moment, Tony squeezed through a dancing couple who both gave him dirty looks. "Sorry," he told them both, executing a small bow. "I just had to move to the tunes, and you were both such excellent dancers that I chose to be with you."

The girl grinned, but the guy's jaw clamped tight.

"Sometimes that fast talk doesn't quite work," Matt told him, grinning as he clapped Tony on the back.

"It works on the ladies." Tony grinned outrageously. "Hey, man, hand over some twisty fries."

Matt uncoiled the last strand and gave it to Tony, who proceeded to eat it as if he were a sword swallower.

Jenny's gaze turned back to Tiffani and Drew as if drawn by a magnet. *Matt's right,* she thought. *I've got to get over this.*

Tiffani closed her eyes and smiled, her head resting lightly against Drew's broad chest as they swayed together gently. This was heaven! She was so lucky to have found him.

"My planets must be in perfect alignment," she murmured blissfully. "This is so cool!"

"Yeah?" Drew looked down at her blond head of hair.

Tiffani peeked upward. "Don't you think it was fate that we met? If I hadn't knocked you over with my surfboard, who knows what could have happened!"

"Yeah." He nodded.

"I wasn't even planning to be at that surfing competition, but I decided to go at the last minute." She giggled, shaking her head. "Isn't it amazing! There you were with Caroline Newsome from my school, and she introduced us and told you I was part of California Dreams! If all that hadn't happened, we would have never realized how many things we had in common!"

"Yeah."

"We could have passed by each other like two ships in the night." She thrust out an arm dramatically. "Two souls, searching for love, never to find each other. . . ."

"You want some twisty fries?" Drew asked.

"Sure," Tiffani agreed.

Drew grabbed her hand and zigzagged ahead of her through the crowd on the way to the snack stand. Tiffani half ran to keep pace. "I forgot how you said you and Caroline met," she yelled above the noise to him.

"Just by chance. Like you and me."

Tiffani's brow puckered as she came up beside him in front of the booth. "On the beach?"

"Uh . . . yeah. I think I'll have a dog, too. You want one?"

"I'll settle for a soda and fries."

Drew bought the sodas, hot dog, and fries; then he and Tiffani headed away from the street dance and toward the beach. The music slowly slid to the background, replaced by the roar of the ocean. Tiffani wound one arm through Drew's. After tossing her paper cup and the rest of her fries into a trash bin, she yanked off her sandals and, holding them in one hand, let her toes squish in the cool, night sand. Drew followed suit, and they walked toward the water's edge. Waves lapped at their feet and swept in brisk swells up their legs.

Tiffani was glad she'd worn her shorts, but the night breeze was a little chilly and so she was even more glad for Drew's strong, warm arm.

"This is great, huh?" he asked.

"Fabu, as Jenny says," Tiffani agreed with a squeaky laugh. "Brrr! The water's a little cold!"

Drew's arm tightened and Tiffani cuddled closer. "Wow, does Jenny have a great voice," he said reflectively. "You, too."

"Thanks."

"Who sings more songs, you or Jenny?"

"It's pretty even, I guess. When Matt writes a song that he wants sung by one of us, he just lets us work it out together. Tony and Matt share songs, too."

"I like that one she sang on the tape."

" 'Cross My Heart'?"

"Yeah, I think that was it."

"It's really great," Tiffani agreed, loving the moment. Drew was really special. She'd dated a lot of guys, some who understood her interest in music, most who didn't. But Drew was perfect, with a capital *P*!

"Do you ever worry that since Jenny's Matt's sister that she might . . ." He let his voice trail off as he stopped walking and gazed down at her.

"What?"

"I don't know. Get more attention?"

"Oh, no! Matt is so fair. I mean, he's really

59

fair. He'd never hurt anybody and neither would Jenny. They're just absolutely the best. I wish there was room for you in the band. I really do," she added sincerely, her face clouding over as she remembered his disappointment.

"Oh, hey, it's okay." His hands slid up her shoulders and cupped her chin, turning her face to his. Tiffani waited breathlessly. She'd kissed Drew a few times, but so far, it had been light, little affectionate pecks like you'd give a good friend. She could tell this was going to be something special!

"You're my girl, aren't you?" he murmured.

Tiffani smiled in anticipation. "Soul mates," she whispered.

"Yeah. Soul mates. I like that."

He bent his head to hers, his mouth gently touching her lips, softly at first and then with deepening intensity. Soul-stirring intensity, she decided, her heart thumping. Wrapping her arms around his neck, she returned his kiss eagerly, a little thrill chasing down her spine.

After what felt like an eternity, he pulled back, gazing deeply into her eyes. "Soul friends," he said.

"Soul mates," she corrected with a contented sigh.

"Yeah, yeah. Soul mates."

He kissed her again; then Tiffani sighed and laid her head against his broad chest, eyes closed.

"Someday, I'm going to be the lead singer in my own band," Drew said as they started back to the street dance.

She bobbed her head enthusiastically. "I know you will! You're really going places. It'll all fall together. You just have to have a positive attitude."

"Right. This is perfect, huh?"

"Perfect," Tiffani giggled with satisfaction.

Jenny swirled her ice cubes around within her paper cup. The band was on break, and the center of the street had opened up a little. She was standing in front of the currently empty bandstand—and feeling blue. Tiffani and Drew had headed for the beach half an hour earlier, and it was a good bet that they were enjoying some quality time together.

"Hey," Matt said in her ear.

Jenny turned around. Out of the corner of her eye she saw Tony, who'd struck up a conversation with the girl whose dance he'd interrupted earlier. The girl's date was glaring daggers from ten feet away.

"Wicks strikes again," Jenny murmured.

Matt glanced at Tony. "He'd better hope someone doesn't strike at him. Where're Tiffani and Drew?"

"Looks like they went for a stroll on the beach."

"Hmmm." Matt sounded noncommittal, but Jenny could practically hear the thoughts churning inside his head. Choosing to ignore him, she sauntered in the direction of the beach.

"Where're you going?" Matt demanded behind her.

"I'm just hanging around." Jenny was defensive.

"Jenny!" Matt's handsome face was concerned. "Stop acting so weird."

"You're overreacting."

"Tony's not the only one who's living dangerously," Matt protested. "You were about to follow your best friend on a date."

"Oh, I was not!"

"Am I the only one here with any sense?" he asked. At that moment, his gaze fell on someone across the street and he sucked in a breath.

"What?" Jenny asked.

"It's Randi Jo," he said distractedly.

Jenny's gaze matched her brother's. Randi Jo, a slim, elegant blond with a friendly smile, was standing to one side, talking with a huge, dark-haired guy. Her long hair was clipped to one side, and she was wearing an emerald green tunic over black stretch pants. She looked absolutely terrific, and by Matt's admiring expression, Jenny was pretty sure he thought so, too.

"I think I'll go talk to her." He took two steps

in Randi Jo's direction before Jenny grabbed his arm and swung him around.

"Am I the only one here with any sense?" she mimicked.

"Yeah, but she's my girlfriend!"

"Ex-girlfriend," Jenny reminded him. "Matt, that guy's her date. If you go over there, it'll be a disaster."

"I just want to talk to her."

"No, Matt. Wait . . ."

Too late. Matt was already striding through the throng to Randi Jo. Jenny sighed. Hearing the first notes of a guitar, she glanced up. Solar Energy was tuning up for the second set.

"Where's Matt?" Tony asked, appearing at Jenny's side as the band really got into gear.

She pointed. Matt had joined Randi Jo and her date. The "date," whose muscles outranked even Drew's, was looking at Matt as if he were his next meal.

"Uh-oh." Tony made a face. "Bad vibes."

"How are you doing with the girl you 'poached,' to use Matt's phrase?" Jenny asked.

"Poached? I was just showing her the patented Tony Wicks slide-and-glide moves." At her look, he added quickly, "*Dance* moves. Whirl-and-twirl. That kind of thing."

"Sure." Jenny swallowed a laugh.

Tony pretended to be sensitive. "I would

never take a foxy babe away from her partner."

"Unless it was easy."

"Well . . ." Tony flashed her a grin. "Yeah."

"Uh-oh," Jenny murmured, seeing Matt with Randi Jo in the middle of the street, wrapped close together and swaying to a slow dance.

Tony glanced from Matt to Randi Jo's date, whose face was a storm cloud. He whistled slowly. "Trouble."

Matt filled his lungs with the sweet scent of Randi Jo's perfume. It was so great to hold her in his arms again. They'd been apart too long.

"Matt," Randi Jo protested.

"What?" He looked down at her. Her blue eyes were full of doubts.

"You shouldn't have pulled me out here. I'm here with Michael."

"It's just one dance."

When he and Randi Jo had split up, Matt had had mixed emotions. A part of him had forced the break up, but another part had been sorry when it happened. They'd sworn they would stay friends, and, for the most part, they had. But seeing her with this Michael guy . . . Matt was sure this "friends stuff" was for the birds.

"Okay, you!" A huge hand clamped down on Matt's shoulder and spun him around just as the song ended in a final chord.

"Hey!" Matt responded, annoyed.

Randi Jo's Michael glared at him, and a corner of his mouth quivered as if he wanted to snarl. Matt stood his ground, but his stomach sank. The last thing he wanted was a fight.

"Look . . . ," he started, but Michael suddenly shoved him hard. Matt tumbled into a group of people, who gasped in surprise.

"Come on, jerk. Let's do it!" Michael invited, beckoning Matt with waving fingers that stuck out from two hammy fists.

"Michael, don't!" Randi Jo cried.

"Stay out of this, Randi Jo," Matt ordered, struggling to his feet.

Michael growled, "You're mine!"

"Michael!" Randi Jo screamed.

He lunged forward and Matt sidestepped him. The crowd moved back, making room. Examining Michael's bulk and angry eyes, Matt decided to use brains instead of brawn. "Maybe we can talk this out," he suggested. Michael's answer was to clamp one hammy fist around Matt's windpipe. "Then again, maybe not!" Matt squeaked out.

"Hey, everybody! Let's dance!" a familiar voice rang out over the loudspeaker. "It's time to slide and it's time to glide. Grab a partner and move!"

Out of the corner of his eye, Matt saw Tony onstage. Tony whipped around in a fast circle, ignoring the surprised looks from Solar Energy. "Do you want to dance?" he yelled into the microphone. "Let's get heated up!"

"Yeah!" the mob responded.

"I can't hear you!" Tony cupped his ear with a hand.

"Yeah!" they boomed back.

The grip on Matt's throat loosened. He gasped and choked and coughed, and finally dragged in a ragged breath. Michael's head was rocking to Tony's impromptu act.

"Later," Michael barked out to Matt. Grabbing Randi Jo's hand, he whipped her into his beefy arms.

Matt gazed after them, half inclined to interrupt them again. Who did this jerk think he was?

"Aren't you the guy who told me to get a life?" Jenny asked innocently, coming up beside him.

Matt snorted in disgust just as Drew and Tiffani returned. Jenny felt her heart skip a beat and fought to pretend not to notice.

"What's Tony doing?" Tiffani asked, getting into the rhythm of Tony's song.

"Don't ask," Matt muttered, stalking away.

"Saving Matt," Jenny said.

Tiffani gazed at her blankly, and Drew said, "Think we could finish that dance now?"

It took Jenny a moment to realize he was talking to her. "Uh . . . sure."

Before she knew it, Drew had whisked her into the crowd, and then they were both moving to Tony's fast hip-talking rap-and-dance happening. (Or so Tony labeled it over the microphone!)

Pretty soon, Solar Energy took the microphone away from Tony and slid into a slow ballad. Drew swept Jenny close, and she couldn't help but notice the shirt button straining below his neck. "So you and Tiffani went to the beach?"

He nodded. Jenny could feel the bulk of his muscles every time he moved. *Not my kind of guy at all,* she reminded herself. "You work out or something?" she guessed.

"Yeah. I'm into bodybuilding."

Good grief. Another zero ambition. What is wrong with me?

Jenny shook her head and glanced to the sidelines. Tiffani was watching them, her face reflecting confusion and worry. Jenny quickly ended the dance and rejoined Tiffani and Matt just as Sly showed up.

"Guess what?" Sly announced, adjusting the cuffs of his neon blue jacket.

"What?" Tony asked as he joined them. Matt slapped his hand and muttered, "Thanks, man," grimacing a little.

Sly inhaled a long breath and let it out slowly, a smile spreading across his face. "Now, don't all hug me at once, but I've got the news you've all been waiting for."

"You've had a personality transplant?" Jenny asked.

"Very funny. Laugh now, but cry tears of joy next. As of this afternoon, *I've* got a record label interested in the band!"

Chapter 6

For a long, long, *long* moment, no one said anything. "What is this?" Sly demanded. "I give you the best news of the Dreams' career and you act like someone's turned off the volume? Speak!"

"A recording label?" Matt asked. "A *real* recording label?"

"No, a fake one." Sly sighed in exasperation. "Of course a real recording label!"

"Do you mean it?" Tiffani asked hopefully, turning to Drew as her face lit up with excitement.

"Yes, I mean it!"

"Wow," Tony commented, then looked skeptical.

"Which recording label?" Jenny asked.

"Now, now, now. All in good time."

"It's a scam." She started to stalk away, and Sly hurried to catch up to her.

"Jenny, Jenny, Jenny . . . would I steer you wrong?"

Jenny stopped to stare him right in the eye. "Only left when the sign reads right, Winkle."

"Okay, I admit there might have been a few minor incidents in the past where you could have gotten the idea that I'd—"

"Screwed up?"

Sly threw an arm across her shoulders, guiding her back to the mass of people in the middle of the street. Solar Energy was really pumping and the music throbbed. This was Sly's opportunity to show Jenny his best moves, and he wasn't going to blow it.

"What do you think you're doing?" she demanded when he pulled her tightly into his arms and spun her out to arm's length, only to pull her back again. Jenny's natural rhythm and litheness kept her from tripping over the couple he'd inadvertently thrown her into.

"Sorry."

"Let go of me!"

"Wait, Jen. Watch this!"

With all the Dreams' attention focused on him, Sly jumped down on his hands and then popped back up. Pumped up, he leaped into the air, intending to land in a splits—or a facsimile thereof—but one foot twisted beneath him and Sly slammed onto his hip with a jolt.

"Are you all right?" Jenny was there in a flash, leaning over him, hands reaching down for him.

If there was ever an opportunity to lay a lipper on her, this was it. Sly looked up, stared into her concerned brown eyes, and moved in for the kill.

With a screech Jenny jumped up. Her shoulder connected with Sly's chin and he saw stars. *Love hurts,* he thought dazedly as Tony and Matt hauled him to his feet.

"You gonna be all right, Winkle?" Tony asked, dusting off Sly's jacket.

"Yeah."

"If you ever do that again, I'll take out your tongue and tie it in a knot!" Jenny declared.

"So, which recording label is interested in us?" Matt asked once they'd helped Sly to a folding chair. Drew leaned forward, eager to hear Sly's response.

"It's . . . um . . ."

"Um?" Tiffani encouraged.

"Um," Sly repeated, looking from Jenny's skeptical face to Tiffani's eager one. "BBG Records."

"What!?" Jenny shrieked as they all grimaced as if on cue.

"BBG has some unqualified hits. And

they've *made* some bands all on their own," Sly defended them.

"The Breathsprays?" Tony declared incredulously. "That's not a band, that's a product!"

"One maybe Sly ought to invest in," Jenny added.

"Now, now, let's not get nasty." Sly winced and held his jaw, and a flash of concern crossed Jenny's mobile features. *It works,* Sly thought, adding a groan for good measure.

"How interested are they in us?" Jenny wanted to know.

"BBG himself requested the demo tape," Sly told her triumphantly.

"Really?" Matt, who'd been standing back, started to show interest.

"We really sound good on the demo," Tiffani pointed out.

"Wow," Drew said, staring at Sly with new respect.

Growing confident, Sly climbed to his feet, surveying all of them. "And just wait until BBG hears some of California Dreams' other songs. While we're recording them, in *his* studio. Face it, guys, Sly Winkle has pulled another rabbit out of a hat. And we're all about to make music history!"

"Are you sure?" Tony asked.

"BBG and I are close, man," Sly went on. "I'll

call him up and arrange a meeting. Okay?"

Everyone agreed, although somewhat reluctantly. They'd had their hopes dashed before when the demo hadn't gotten any airtime. Still, BBG Records *was* a recording label. . . .

Sly could see they were starting to come around. His smile was broad, but niggling doubts invaded his mind. What would happen when the Dreams met BBG in the flesh? And why did he keep envisioning some kind of disaster?

A week later, the Dreams assembled at Sharkey's for their meeting with Brad Bartley Griffin, Jr. Tony served all of them burgers, fries, and shakes, and when Sharkey looked over at their table, Tony flashed him an "I told you so" grin that sent Sharkey muttering back to the kitchen.

"No way the Sharkman can fire me now," Tony declared, flipping a chair around and straddling it backward.

"Aren't you supposed to be working?" Sly pointed out.

"I'm on break, man. Besides, I gotta be here when the big man arrives."

"I think he just walked in," Tiffani whispered as a young man with slicked-down hair and an Armani suit stepped inside the burger joint, glanced around in distaste, then spied Sly's frantically waving arm. He stepped tentatively around the tables, as if fearing his Italian leather shoes might land in something noxious.

Jenny was offended. Sharkey's wasn't the Café Ritz but, hey! It was a great place. She disliked BBG already.

"All right, listen, kids," he jumped in almost before Sly had finished making introductions. "You're something special. You've got a sound, y'know. The kind of thing that sells and sells big."

"Gosh, you really think so!" Tiffani squeezed Jenny's arm excitedly.

BBG flicked her a look. "I'm ready to go professional. The question is, are you ready for it?"

"You bet!" Tony cried, leaping from his chair.

"What do you mean by that, exactly?" Matt asked cautiously.

"We'll cut an album. Make a cassette and CD. We'll sell you like no group's been sold before! I am talking mega-stardom. Concerts. Road tours. The works!"

"Wait until I tell Drew!" Tiffani squealed. "He'll go crazy!"

"But you've only heard one of our songs," Jenny broke in. "How can you tell—"

"Listen, kid, when you've been in this business as long as I have, you just know."

Since he looked about two years older than she

was, Jenny couldn't help having some doubts.

"California Dreams could be bigger than the Breathsprays," he added in a confidential voice. "Bigger even than Tinker and the Bells."

If he'd expected this announcement to fuel their enthusiasm, he was disappointed. Jenny looked at Matt, who looked at Tony, who looked at Tiffani, who looked at Sly.

"Well?" Sly asked, mustering up an excited grin.

"Well . . . okay," Matt said, extending his hand to BBG.

BBG shook Matt's hand and then smoothed his tie. He gave all of them long looks, his gaze lingering on Tiffani. "You won't be sorry," he said, "although there are naturally going to be a few minor changes in the band's format."

"What kind of changes?" Matt demanded instantly.

"Nothing to worry about. Just show up at BBG Records Monday afternoon, and we'll put the wheels on this vehicle."

After BBG left the Dreams, they all stared at each other. Finally Sly said, "What did I tell you? We're on the road to the big time, and you know who to thank."

"Or who to blame," Jenny responded dourly.

● ● ●

The recording studio itself was as slick as the rest of BBG Records' building decor. Jenny, Matt, Tony, and Tiffani set up their instruments and waited for guidance. Sly stood to one side, surveying the scene like a conquering hero. He ignored the butterflies in his stomach. He just wished he could ignore Drew Wylde with the same steely concentration, but since Drew was standing right beside him, an invited guest at Tiffani's request, it was hard to pretend he was invisible.

The side door opened with a bang, and BBG strolled in, a red-haired man in jeans and a sweatshirt keeping in step with him.

"I'd like to hear the openings to a couple of your songs," BBG announced to the group at large. "Just play a few bars and we'll see what happens."

"Okay . . ." Matt picked out a few songs and cued Tony, Jenny, and Tiffani on which notes to start on. He broke into the first song, but when Jenny came in with the vocals, BBG cut her off.

"Next," he ordered.

The Dreams started their second song—and the same thing happened. The third song was a solo by Matt, and BBG listened to that for an extra couple of bars.

"Okay, okay," he said, waving them to stop as his red-haired companion wrote furiously in a notebook. "We've got too many female vocals here. We'll have to cut back."

"What?" Matt asked, scarcely believing his ears.

"I want to make this a more male sound. Y' know, we're California Dreams. We're dreamin' of California girls!"

"We can't cut out Jenny and Tiffani," Tony protested.

"No, no, no." BBG walked over to Jenny. "We just want to change the balance a little, that's all."

"BBG . . ." Sly sauntered over to the studio owner. "Maybe if you heard all the songs, you'd see that—"

"I know what I'm talking about, Mr. Sly," BBG interrupted. He turned his attention to Jenny. "You want to cut an album, babe? We've just got to fix things a little."

Babe? Jenny mouthed to Matt. Matt shook his head and lifted his palms in surrender.

"You've got a great voice, honey," BBG added silkily, looking Jenny over.

She stared him straight in the eye. "Don't tell me. Let me guess: We could make beautiful music together."

BBG laughed. "Cute. Real cute."

Sly hurried to intercede. He could tell Jenny wanted to pack it in. But the look Jenny shot him stopped him cold, and he merely stood by anxiously, wondering who BBG would insult next.

"Nice hair," BBG said to Tiffani, examining

her shining blond mane critically. "It'll look good on-camera." The onceover he gave her was frankly appreciative.

"On-camera?" Tiffani asked.

"When we shoot the video," BBG told her.

Tiffani's eyes widened in surprised delight. "The video. Cool!"

"Why don't I tell you more at dinner tonight?" BBG suggested.

Jenny bristled. She opened her mouth to tell this sleaze bag where to get off when Tiffani, in her most Tiffani way, saved the day. "Would it be all right if Drew came with us?" she asked eagerly. "This is just so . . . wow!"

"Drew?" BBG looked annoyed.

On cue, Drew joined them in the center of the room. His easy smile calmed Jenny down instantly. There was something about him that just—worked.

"Drew Wylde. My boyfriend," Tiffani introduced.

"This is the coolest," Drew told BBG earnestly, shaking his hand. "I tried out with California Dreams, and they just didn't need me, but one of these days . . ."

"You tried out? As a band member?" BBG asked, his attention sharpening.

"Oh, yeah." Drew shrugged modestly. "I sing and play a little guitar."

"No kidding." BBG stroked his chin reflectively and then spun around slowly, surveying the entire band. His red-haired friend whispered something into his ear, and BBG nodded as if he'd come to the same conclusion. "We're going to add Drew to the band."

Jenny and Tiffani gasped. Matt's jaw sank. Tony dropped his drumsticks, and Sly sputtered out, "You've got to be kidding!"

"He's perfect. He looks *fabulous*. Long blond hair. Built like a muscleman. The kid's a California Dream himself!" BBG's eyes shone with excitement. "Can't you see it? A volleyball video on the beach with Drew front and center." He chortled with delight and clapped Drew's hand in his as if they were long-lost buddies.

"You mean it!" Drew blinked at his good fortune.

"That song . . . that song . . ." BBG snapped his fingers. "The one where Jenny-babe sings lead. Let's work it around for Drew."

"Now, wait a minute," Matt interjected, unstrapping his guitar.

"No, it's okay," Jenny cut in quickly. She was burned, and a little hurt, but if this was what it would take to cut an album, she was willing to make sacrifices. And she didn't really mind as much because Drew would benefit. Maybe he would become a permanent member of the band and that would be okay.

Or at least that's what she told herself.

"I think we should talk about this," Matt said heatedly. "I'm serious. Mr. Griffen, we'll get back to you."

"Whoa-ho!" Sly clapped Matt on the back and jerked him aside. "Don't anger the boss man, Matt. You could blow it."

"Blow it! With Drew in the band? Come on, Sly. This is more than a little bitty change!"

"BBG and I talk the same language. Leave it all to me."

Sly walked back to BBG and said, "As the Dreams' manager, I've been appointed to discuss these changes with you in private."

"Oh, brother," Jenny muttered under her breath. This was going from bad to worse.

"All right, Mr. Sly. Everybody else, I'm going to set up that video taping. Drew, learn the song. Jenny-babe, you can still sing, but I want it background like the blond girl."

"Tiffani," Tiffani told him.

"Whatever." BBG twisted on his heel, and Sly had to run to catch up to him.

"BBG, I don't think Drew is really going to work with California Dreams," Sly said. "He's only rehearsed with us once, and, frankly, he wasn't Dreams material. He was okay, but not that great. You haven't even heard him sing, yet."

"If he's awful, we'll work something out," BBG said flatly.

"What do you mean?"

BBG thrust open the side door. "We'll use his voice as backup vocals."

Sly was amazed. Here was a guy who thought up sleazier schemes than he did! "The Dreams'll never go for it!"

"Oh, yes, they will," BBG said in a low, intense voice meant for Sly's ears alone. "This is what they're going to do if they want to cut an album. Now, are *you* going to tell them, or do I have to?"

Chapter 7

Jenny sat with her chin in her hand, staring out the windows at a lightly falling rain, ignoring the droning voice of Mr. Falk, her English teacher.

The week had started out with a bang. Since meeting with BBG at his recording studio on Monday, the Dreams had been talking and talking and *talking*, but so far, nothing had been decided. The consensus of the band was that Drew should not be part of the group. But according to Sly, BBG was bound and determined that Drew would, indeed, be an important member.

Jenny didn't know how to feel. She'd covered up her hurt because it had seemed like the thing to do, but now she was kind of angry. She was an important part of California Dreams! How could BBG just dump her like that?

Not that he'd totally knocked her out. But adding Drew seemed to be cutting into just *her* songs—at least so far.

Drew.

Jenny sighed and shook her head. He was coming by the house this afternoon to rehearse for the video. She couldn't believe BBG had decreed he would be one of their lead singers when the Dreams had already told him he couldn't be!

And what will it be like, rehearsing with him almost every day? she thought.

Sighing again, she doodled on her notepad. She was supposed to be writing a ballad about the environment, but when she looked at her blank paper, all she could see was Drew's happy, excited face when BBG had promoted him to "Dream" status.

"Miss Garrison," Mr. Falk suddenly cut in. "Would you be kind enough to read what you've written so far?"

Busted! Jenny inhaled in shock and then made a production out of clearing her throat. "Well . . ." The clock ticked loudly, like some finger being waved tsk-tsk in front of her nose. The class grew so quiet, the tiniest cough sounded like an explosion.

"Ummm . . . ," Jenny murmured, sweating.

Inspiration suddenly struck! She'd been listening to Matt plunk away at the piano while he'd fought to compose that new song. It hadn't been going all that well, but Jenny suddenly knew the right rhythm.

With the tune running through her mind, Jenny half sang in ballad form:

> *"Who can you trust with*
> *life's greatest secrets,*
> *Who can you trust when*
> *trust alone is the key?*
> *I can't trust just*
> *anyone—that would be*
> *foolish,*
> *It's got to be someone who*
> *looks out for me."*

Mr. Falk blinked, and then took off his glasses and polished them. "Very good, Ms. Garrison," he muttered in a voice so low it was barely audible. Loudly, he asked, "Ms. Sanders, what have you got?"

Hah! Jenny thought smugly as the class's attention swiveled to Mr. Falk's latest victim. She'd handled Mr. Falk, and she couldn't wait to get home to sing her lyrics to Matt.

Matt slammed his backpack down on the kitchen counter and headed straight for the refrigerator for a soda. Popping the top off the can, he muttered beneath his breath and then nearly jumped a foot when a *whoop-whoop-whoop* siren blasted in his ear.

"Gotcha!" his little brother, Dennis, gleefully shouted.

"Dennis, I swear, if I'd spilled one drop of this drink, I'd pour the rest over your head!"

"What's this?" Mrs. Garrison peeked her head in from the living room.

"I'm threatening Dennis," Matt told her without a shred of remorse.

"You'll never catch me!" Dennis was gone in a clatter of sneakers and more *whoop-whoop-whoop*.

Mrs. Garrison walked into the kitchen, lugging a basket of towels and sheets for the laundry. "What brought on this foul mood?"

Matt followed his mother to the garage and watched as she loaded the washer. "We've got a chance to cut an album. A real album, but the guy in charge is a nightmare. He's more interested in marketing than music, and he wants to change the band. How long is the laundry going to take?"

Mrs. Garrison glanced over her shoulder at the Dreams' equipment, which was already set out and ready in their garage. "Give me an hour and a half and it should be washed and dried, as long as Jenny remembers to put the wash in the dryer on time."

"I'll do it," Matt said, stabbed by another

twinge of guilt. He felt especially bad for Jenny after the way BBG had treated her. What an unbelievable sleaze bag! The guy could win a world record in lowlifeness.

He put the whites into the washer and twisted the knob. His mother's brows lifted. "Since when did you take over Jenny's chores?"

"Since she got the shaft from BBG," Matt muttered.

"Matt!" Jenny's voice called from the kitchen. He looked up as she ran through the open garage door, her face lit up with excitement. "I think I've worked out some lyrics for your new song!" The thump of the washer caught her attention, and she slowed to a stop.

Mrs. Garrison turned off the washer. "We'll do it later," she said with a smile, and then left as Jenny pulled a crumpled piece of paper from her back pocket and smoothed it out on top of the piano.

Matt read through her lyrics aloud. "Not bad."

"It's like a ballad," Jenny enthused. "I had to write one for English and wham-o! It came to me in a flash of inspiration!"

"It's good," Matt said, his interest catching fire. He softly sang the lyrics. "In fact it's great! Perfect for your voice, too."

Jenny was brought up short by the memory of BBG cutting her out of "Cross My Heart."

"Maybe we should wait on that," she murmured. "Until we know exactly what's happening with the band."

"Hi, guys!" Tiffani appeared in the doorway, giving them both a little wave. She looked kind of sheepish as she and Drew entered the garage for their first rehearsal with him on board.

Jenny's gaze zeroed in on Drew, who wasn't wearing a shirt. In fact, the only adornment on his upper torso was a shell necklace and a few scattered raindrops running down his sun-bronzed skin.

Matt cleared his throat several times, as if not sure how to begin. Finally, he asked, "Well, Drew, are you ready?" in a voice that made it clear he didn't like this new arrangement any more than the rest of them did.

"I'm looking forward to it!" Drew responded.

He'd brought his own guitar and, after looking around, squeezed himself between Tiffani and Jenny. That left Matt on the far left and Jenny on the far right. Drew was front and center since Tiffani was dwarfed by his size.

Tony appeared, whistling, but then he froze in midstep as he checked out the new band setup. For once, he chose to keep his fast talk and opinions to himself and wisely only mumbled a few words of greeting before taking his place at the drums.

"How's it going with Sharkey?" Matt asked him, tuning up his guitar.

"Not bad, not bad. Should change his name though, since he's been eyeing me like a *hawk.*"

"He could call his place Hawk-eys!" Tiffani said brightly.

"Hockeys sounds like a sports place," Jenny pointed out, running her fingers through some warm-ups on the keyboard.

"I'm here!" Sly boomed from the doorway, both arms raised as he jumped down the steps into the garage. "And so's Drew," he added more slowly as he, too, eyed the new arrangement.

"We're going to run through 'Cross My Heart,' then onto 'Perfection,' and we'll finish with 'After the Rain,' " Matt told them all.

Jenny noticed he didn't even mention his new song, and she was glad. Maybe it could be just their voices. She could certainly use the boost to her self-esteem!

They ran through each song twice and then everyone turned to Matt, as if waiting for him to make some recommendations. Matt took a deep breath and looked at Drew. "Not bad," he said.

Sly choked out a laugh. Everyone looked at him and he regained his composure. Not bad? Who was Matt kidding? With Drew belting out lead vocals, those three songs were in the toilet!

"Think I'm ready for the video?" Drew asked eagerly, pushing his blond hair out of his eyes. Muscles rippled.

"Let's take a break," Matt suggested.

Sly pulled Matt aside at the first opportunity. "Not bad?" he repeated. *"Not bad?"*

"You're the one who said BBG still wants to use him!" Matt reminded him. "You'd better find a way to change his mind."

Sly grimaced as he watched Drew leave Tiffani to go and say a few words to Jenny. He hadn't been completely honest with the Dreams about BBG's ultimatum. They all thought having Drew in the band was still a matter of choice.

"Maybe he'll improve," Sly said hopefully.

Matt snorted. "By the end of the week? Fat chance."

Tiffani bopped over to them. "Having Drew in the band makes it different, doesn't it?" she asked, her smile a little strained. "But he's pretty good, isn't he?"

"Pretty good," Matt agreed diplomatically.

"He stinks," Sly said.

Tiffani turned on him. "That's not fair! It's not Drew's fault that that creep at the studio wants us to include him."

Tony joined their group. "Hey, Matt, why'd

you have Drew sing the songs where you're the lead? It's not right, man. We can all give up some tunes."

"I just didn't like the way BBG started cutting out the girls," Matt said.

"Yeah, well, if you don't watch yourself, you'll find that yo-yo will be cutting you out next!"

"No!" Tiffani was emphatic. "BBG will never cut out Matt. He's the brains behind the band, the songwriter. The heart of the group. Matt *is* the Dreams!"

"For once I agree with you," Sly said. "BBG won't sacrifice the band."

Oh, yeah? Matt thought, but he didn't voice his thoughts. He looked over at Jenny and Drew, and his heart sank still lower as he saw the glowing happiness on his sister's face as she gazed up at the newest addition to California Dreams.

"You really think I was okay, then?" Drew asked Jenny for about the fifth time.

"More than okay," she responded, feeling a bit like Benedict Arnold because each time she'd answered him, her voice had grown less and less convincing.

"I think I really got into 'Perfection.' I like all that stuff about how people look. Image. It's important."

Jenny's smile faltered. The song was about all

the problems there were when a person sought perfection. Its message was clearly "Be yourself, not some image that's out of reach." She didn't think Drew had got into "Perfection" quite the way he believed.

"Tiffani really wants this to work out," Drew said when Jenny remained silent.

"We all do." Jenny's voice was quiet, because she knew the way she and the rest of the Dreams felt was in direct opposition to how Drew performed.

She didn't want Drew in the band. That didn't mean she didn't like him; she did, but he just wasn't right for the Dreams.

And they all knew it. Even Tiffani.

"This is going to be great!" He grinned happily.

"Drew . . . ," Jenny murmured.

"I've got some ideas for songs. Good ones. I've been working on them."

"Maybe you ought to wait on that. . . ."

"Wait! Why?" He gazed at her through innocent eyes.

Jenny swallowed hard. She'd never been one to shirk from a thorny problem, and she couldn't now. It was too important to everyone involved. "Drew, I really like you. We all do, so don't take this the wrong way, okay?"

He waited, confused.

"Your sound isn't quite right for California

91

Dreams," she said as Sly, Tony, Matt, and Tiffani walked within earshot.

"What do you mean?" Drew asked, stunned.

"I guess what I'm saying is that we're complete on our own. BBG may not understand that yet, but I think we can convince him—with your help."

"Gee . . ." Drew's handsome forehead creased in heavy-duty thought.

Feeling miserable, Jenny added in a small voice, "Please don't take this personally."

No one knew what to say, which made Jenny feel worse. It didn't help that she could see how much she'd hurt his feelings.

"I'll have to think about this," Drew said as he went to pick up his equipment.

"And burn up his only two working brain cells?" Sly muttered beneath his breath.

Jenny elbowed him, and Tiffani shot him a dirty look as she headed over to join Drew.

"Good work," Matt told Jenny, giving her a light hug. "I know that was tough."

"I just said what we were all thinking."

"And how," Sly agreed with gusto.

Jenny's eyes narrowed to furious slits. "Zip it, Winkle."

"Do you think he'll quit, like, voluntarily?" Tony asked, sending a dubious look Drew's way. "I mean, he really seemed to be into the fast track to glitz and glory."

"Time will tell," Matt said.

Jenny sighed. She'd done the right thing, but that didn't make her feel any better, nor did it mean she'd gotten over her feelings for Drew.

At that very moment, Drew glanced up and sent her a long, searching look that did strange things to her insides. She hoped he wouldn't blame her for being the one to ask him to leave California Dreams. She felt bad enough as it was.

Chapter 8

"Jenny!" Sly called, following after her into the Garrisons' kitchen. "I know that was tough."

"Thanks." She really wished she could be left alone so she had time to put her feelings in order.

Sly planted himself on one of the kitchen stools and watched as she heated a pot of tea. "But, you know, I've been thinking."

Jenny slid him a look. "Pace yourself. You have the whole day ahead of you."

"Ha-ha." Sly took no offense. He knew, deep in the center of his manly being, that she wanted him.

He stopped short, ran that line over in his mind a second time, and decided it was good. Really good.

"Jenny, you can't hide from me anymore."

Jenny looked up from the stove top. "Not now, Sly," she said on a sigh. "I'm really not in the mood."

"You want me." He spread his arms wide, letting her get a good look at Sly Winkle, the man.

Jenny didn't know whether to laugh or cry. Sly's timing was always so *wrong*!

"I say we put a hold on this game playing for a while and concentrate on dating," he went on, oblivious to her growing annoyance. "How about tonight? A little dinner, maybe a little dancing, and then later . . ." He built up the suspense. Jenny's brown eyes gazed straight at him. He had her hooked! "*Moi* and a trip to Lovers' Leap. What do you say?"

"Sly . . . babe," she said, advancing on him. "The only way I'll ever go to Lovers' Leap is if you leap over it!"

The door opened and Tiffani burst in, followed by Tony, Matt, and Drew. Jenny instantly went back to her tea.

She's toying with me, Sly thought. *I love it!*

"I've got to head home and catch up on some homework," Tiffani announced, gazing expectantly at Drew, who hadn't seemed to have heard her.

"Me, too," Tony said. "Gotta work on my math. Sharkey still isn't convinced that I'm the best, the most happening, the ultimate waiter in the place. Gotta increase profit per order." He rubbed his chin thoughtfully on the way out.

"I'll see you later, then?" Tiffani asked Drew, since he still didn't appear to have heard her.

"Sure." He walked her to the door. Tiffani dallied a bit. Then she shrugged, lifted up on tiptoes for a brief kiss good-bye, waved at Jenny, and then left.

Sly was still gazing dreamily at Jenny. "After we make the video, Jenny . . ." He pointed to her and then himself, clearly planning their "date."

"Save me," Jenny muttered beneath her breath as Sly strutted out the door, throwing her an "I'll see you later" look.

Matt pulled Jenny aside. "I take back everything I said about you and Drew," he whispered to her.

"Really?" she asked in surprise.

"Hey, you let him know there was no place for him in the band. Nice going. You've got your priorities in line, after all. Forget about the extra chores. You've paid your dues. I'm proud of ya, kid." He rubbed his knuckles under her chin and headed up to his room.

Jenny felt like a heel. Matt didn't understand. She was rotten through and through, because in spite of everything, the most important thing on her mind right now was that she was finally alone with Drew!

Drew sat down at the counter. Jenny felt shy—an unusual state since she was normally outgoing to the point of brashness.

"Want a cup of tea or hot chocolate?" she asked.

"Got any instant coffee?"

"Sure. How do you like it?"

"Sugar, cream, maybe some chocolate syrup, dash of nutmeg." Drew shrugged. "Don't put a lot of trouble into it."

Jenny bit back a smile. "No trouble at all," she said, but Drew missed the irony.

"I've been meaning to talk to you," he said, stirring the concoction Jenny set in front of him. She sipped a cup of plain tea.

"Yeah?"

"I've got a confession to make." He looked up, his green eyes deep with some suppressed emotion. *Sean had green eyes,* Jenny remembered with a faint pang. "Tiffani and I . . . I thought we had something special . . . that we were soul friends."

"Soul mates?" Jenny asked softly, her heart twisting a bit. She sensed where this was going.

"Yeah, right." He brushed that aside. "Anyway, I was wrong. I mean, I really like Tiffani a lot. She's so cute and . . ." He looked to her for help.

"Bright, bubbly, and full of sparkle?"

"Yeah, that's it! But we're off track, kind of, and I really need someone who's more . . .

more . . ." His green eyes gazed deeply into Jenny's.

"More realistic, focused, and down-to-earth?" she whispered. She could drown in those eyes.

"Right!" He reached a hand across the counter, touching her fingers.

A jolt swept through her, half excitement, half guilt. She was afraid to move, perched on the knife's edge of temptation. This was her chance. He'd already admitted Tiffani wasn't the one for him.

But Tiffani was her best friend, for crying out loud!

"Drew," she managed in a silly, breathless voice totally unlike her usual one. "If you're heading where I think you're heading . . . I can't."

"Why not? I'll tell Tiffani the truth."

"No, it's not right!"

"Jenny . . ." He set down his cup and came around the counter, stopping mere inches from her. She remembered being held in his arms as they'd danced. Remembered loving that feeling of being protected. She wanted to feel that way again.

He lifted her chin until she was forced to meet his gaze. "You're my girl, aren't you?" he said in a low, sexy tone.

Jenny's tongue circled her lips. "I—I don't know."

"Jenny!" Matt called, and she jumped away from Drew as if burned. Matt clambered downstairs, taking the last three steps in a jump. "I've been thinking about the song. Got a minute? I'd love to work on it together."

"Sure." Noisily, she gathered up her and Drew's cups and put them in the sink. Drew gave her a long, knowing look, a smile hovering on his lips.

"See you both at the studio next week," he said as he left.

Matt's jaw dropped. "What? Didn't he get the message?"

"I guess not." Jenny was a little surprised, too, but inside, a small part of her was secretly glad. He didn't blame her for her bluntness. True, he hadn't understood, really, but so what? "When BBG hears him, he'll drop Drew," she soothed Matt. "Sly even said as much."

"And you trust *Sly*?" Matt was incredulous.

"It'll all work out," Jenny predicted. "Just wait and see."

Sly paced outside the room at Coastal Sounds where his cousin Charlie was doing the final mix on another group's demo. No matter how confident Sly had sounded to the Dreams, his stomach was twisted in knots. BBG's radical changes couldn't happen. Sly had to stop him, but he needed ammunition. Ergo, he'd dropped in on good old Charlie, who knew BBG personally.

The door flew open, and Charlie stepped into the hall. His expression darkened as soon as he saw Sly.

"Hey, cousin!" Sly greeted him cheerily.

"What do you want now?"

"Nothing! Whoa! Chill, Charles. I just want to connect and talk a bit, that's all."

"Make it fast. I don't have a lot of time."

Sly hurried to catch up with Charlie's longer strides as they headed down the carpeted hallway. "BBG wants to record California Dreams."

Charlie halted as if stopped short by a choke chain. His eyes sparkled with humor as he turned to Sly. "No kidding!"

"No kidding. What's the joke?"

"Hey, if you can't figure it out." Charlie shook his head.

"Well, there is a slight problem. BBG wants to make some heavy-duty changes. He's grabbed Tiffani's boyfriend, who's got a lot of space upstairs, if you know what I mean." Sly pointed to his head. "BBG wants *him* front and center because he looks like Muscle Beach!"

Charlie's smile disappeared. "Don't do it."

"Of course we're not going to do it." Sly snorted. "What do you take me for?"

"Listen, Sly. I was really torked over that money mess with the demo for your friends, but they have a great sound. And they seemed like nice kids. I don't want to see them get hurt."

"Get hurt?" Sly laughed. "You make it sound like BBG's the new Al Capone."

"He's a sleaze bag with his own agenda. I let you go to him because I wanted you to get your just desserts. But BBG's way beyond 'just desserts.' He won't stop messing with the Dreams until he's re-vamped the band to the point where you won't even recognize it! Have you signed any contracts yet?" he asked anxiously.

"Well . . . no . . ."

"Don't! You'll be signing your life away. Read the fine print and then read it again. BBG's a taker."

"Thanks for the advice, Charlie, but it's not that bad."

"It's a nightmare," Charlie warned intensely. "Go back to the Dreams and tell them to get out! I'm sorry I ever encouraged you to meet with BBG. Trust me, Sly. If you sign with BBG Records, it'll be the worst mistake of your life!"

Chapter 9

"**Y**oo-hoo, Jenny!" Matt waved his hand in front of her face. Her eyes were glazed over and had a faraway look in them. Matt had been trying to keep her attention on the song, but she was somewhere else.

As if coming out of a trance, Jenny jerked. She gazed around blankly, as if she couldn't remember that she and Matt were in the garage, at the piano, working on their song.

"Yeah?" she asked.

"What planet were you visiting?" he asked. "We're working here, right?"

"Sure, sure. I'm just kind of distracted."

"*Kind* of?" Matt laughed.

Jenny put her mind on the task at hand, and they managed to have over an hour of intense, concentrated work before they took a break. Even so, she was glad when they were finished, because Matt's eyes saw too much and his questions scraped too close to the bone. Did he suspect what had happened with Drew?

This wouldn't be the first time she and Matt had disagreed about a guy she was attracted to. She and Matt had been at loggerheads over her relationship with Sean, at least in the beginning. They'd fought and made each other's lives miserable. She didn't want that to happen again. She liked having her brother think she'd been heroic in explaining the truth to Drew. What would his feelings be if he learned the truth?

"Want to talk about it?" Matt asked as they headed to the kitchen and Matt pulled two sodas out of the refrigerator.

Jenny sat at the table with her homework. She bit her lip. "You won't like it."

"Try me." He placed a can of cola in front of her.

At that moment, they heard a car drive in. A few minutes later, Dennis exploded through the back door, followed more sedately by their mother.

"Your dad'll be home soon," Mrs. Garrison said, hefting several bags of groceries onto the counter. "What do you want for dinner?"

"Pizza!" Dennis crowed.

"I meant something I could make," she answered with a smile. "We could have spaghetti, hamburgers, or I could bake a chicken. Name your pleasure."

"Chicken," Jenny said.

"Spaghetti," Matt answered at the same moment.

"Hamburgers!" Dennis chimed in.

"Forget I asked," Mrs. Garrison said. "Tonight it's Mom's choice."

Dennis groaned, hunched over as if the weight of the world were on his shoulders, and stomped out of the kitchen. Mrs. Garrison began putting groceries away, and Jenny got up to help her. Matt's gaze followed his sister's every move.

"Well?" he finally asked.

Jenny wasn't certain she was ready for true confessions. She mumbled an excuse, packed up her books, and then headed upstairs to the privacy of her room. Dumping the books on her desk, she sank into the swivel chair, switched on the desk light, and promptly fell into a delicious daydream:

She and Drew were swimming in a huge pool. Brightly colored umbrellas poked out from shiny white tables, a ring of bright color circling the pool. It was hot. The sky was high and dusty blue. Not a soul was around. Drew swam over to her and murmured in her ear, "Soul friends."

Wrong!

Jenny dismissed that fantasy and moved on to

another one. She and Drew were at a mountain lodge. A fire roared in a huge, stone fireplace big enough to walk into. Woven rugs with Native American designs adorned the hewn, brown fir walls. Drew pulled her close and murmured in her ear, "You're my girl, aren't you? We'll make beautiful music together."

"Yech!" Jenny muttered, annoyed with herself. *What's wrong with this picture?* she asked herself, truly baffled.

A rap sounded at her door. "Enter," she announced.

Matt poked his head inside. "You escaped once, but like the memory of a bad, catchy tune, I keep coming back and back and back. . . ."

"Sit down, Matt," she said with a resigned sigh.

He perched on the end of her bed and looked expectant. Jenny tried to think of a way to approach the subject of Drew without having her brother come unglued. Finally, she just gave up and blurted out, "Drew told me it's just not there with him and Tiffani."

"Not there," Matt repeated, as if he were dense.

"You know, *not there*! Want me to spell it? N-O-T T-H-E—"

"What does he mean by that?" Matt interrupted.

"Well, I think it's pretty clear that he and Tiffani are going to break up."

"And why did he pick you to tell this momentous news? Has he told Tiffani?"

"I don't think so. Not yet, anyway."

"Jenny!"

"What?" she demanded, defensive.

"You told him how you feel, didn't you?"

"No!" Jenny leaped to her feet. "He just said it wasn't there between him and Tiffani. He said that she was too, well, sweet and cute and bubbly, basically."

"And he wants someone sour, ugly, and dull, basically?" Matt asked in a tone Jenny really didn't like.

"You're not even trying to listen." Jenny stomped out of the room and Matt came right after her, dogging her heels all the way to the garage.

"I didn't bring this on, you know! It's not my fault things didn't work out between them!"

"But you're not sorry, are you?"

"Okay, look, Mr. Perfect." Jenny fought back. "You're right, okay? I kind of like Drew and he's admitted that he likes me, too. I'm sorry! I don't want to hurt Tiffani. But Drew can't change his feelings just because it's unfair to Tiffani." She drew a breath. "And neither can I."

"So what are you going to do? Start dating Drew and break Tiffani's heart?"

"I'm not going to do anything!" Jenny practically shouted at him. "I'm just going to stay out of it. I'd really like to date Drew, but I'm not going to risk my friendship with Tiffani. Happy now?"

"What's all the yelling about?" their mother asked as she came into the garage.

Jenny's eyes were shooting daggers at Matt even though she was really mad at herself. What she'd said was the absolute truth. As much as she'd like to date Drew, she couldn't hurt her best friend. And it made her fighting mad!

"Jenny's working through a problem," Matt explained, smothering a smile. "She's using that kind of therapy where you yell and shout a lot."

Mrs. Garrison turned to look at her daughter. Angry as she was, Jenny could see the humor. "It's a primal scream thing," Jenny agreed.

Listening to the thumping washing machine, Mrs. Garrison nodded thoughtfully. "Well, I hope it clears your mind because you just rewashed the clean clothes."

"Oh," Jenny said. Then she and Matt broke into gales of laughter.

Sharkey's was half empty as Sly climbed onto one of the counter stools and ordered a chocolate-pineapple milkshake from one of the blond waitresses.

"Yech," she said as she wrote it down.

"Whoa, whoa, whoa!" Tony appeared as if by magic, snatching the order from her hands and whisking it away. "Mr. Sylvester Winkle is a long-standing customer of mine. No one messes with Tony Wicks's clientele unless they want to flirt with disaster."

"Yeah?" she threw back, unimpressed. "What are you going to do?"

"If you twist the back wire on the jukebox just so"—he turned his fingers as if pinching two wires together—"you can repeat Tinker and the Bells's latest hit over and over again. It's been known to vegify even the brainiest of brains."

The girl snorted and left the order with Tony. Tony read it and said, "Yech."

"None of you appreciate exotic cuisine," Sly muttered, slumping his elbows on the counter.

"What's got you down, man?" Tony asked.

"I've got a small problem," he admitted, remembering his cousin's warning. He frowned. "The good news is: Jenny's finally starting to appreciate all the Winkle charms. Now, if it just wasn't for this bump in the road . . . this wrinkle in the sheet of life."

"Deep," Tony said. "I must've missed Jenny's transformation. Thought you disgusted her."

"No. That's all an act."

"Oscar material, man!" He paused to look at

his friend. "So what's the bump in the road?"

Sly shook his head, and Tony shrugged and went to whip up Sly's shake. Alone, Sly reviewed what Charlie had told him. It couldn't be as bad as he'd made out. This was a tremendous opportunity, not a walk down the plank! Brad Bartley Griffen, Jr., would come around. And Jenny would realize that Sylvester Winkle was the man who'd made her dreams come true.

Why, then, did he feel so nervous?

Tony slid the shake down the counter and Sly caught it on the fly, slurping it down in nearly one long gulp. Tony watched in amazement. "Another?" he asked Sly.

"Just keep 'em coming," Sly responded, checking his pockets for change. Tony eagerly headed for the milk shake machine. Sly watched him whip up another shake and grimaced as Tony slid it in front of him. "Better put it on my tab. I'm a little short at the moment."

Tony yanked the shake away. "Don't get too comfortable," he warned; then he asked the room at large, "Who ordered the chocolate-pine—I mean, Sharkey's special *tropical* shake?"

"What's it got in it?" a male voice yelled back.

"Pineapple . . . pineapple . . . sunshine . . . and chocolate."

"Yech!" the room chorused back.

"Looks like you'll be drinking that one yourself, Wicks," Sharkey's voice blasted in Tony's ear. "And it'll be coming out of this week's pay!"

"Sorry," Sly said to Tony as Sharkey thumped his way back to the kitchen.

"Not as sorry as I am," Tony remarked, taking a huge gulp of Sly's favorite milk shake. His face twisted in agony. He choked. He grabbed his throat. His hands trembled so much he nearly dropped the half-empty glass.

A second later he stood stock-still. "Not bad!" he cried in a voice startled with discovery. Lifting the glass, he stared at it as if it were some miracle potion. "This stuff is great!"

He raised his hand for a high five. Sly complied, and Tony gave his hand a sharp slap. Smiling faintly, Sly watched Tony smack down the rest of the drink.

If only his other problems were solved so easily. Then he'd have reason to celebrate.

Chapter 10

"**M**an, this stuff is great!" Tony said enthusiastically. "It's the shake, rattle, and roll of milk shakes. A tropical, whopical, supremely delicious ice-cream slurpie!"

"Glad you like it," Sly said.

"Like it? I am ready to go nationwide with this. Can't you see it?" Throwing an arm over Sly's shoulders, he spread his hand in front of both of them, opening up a vista of the future. "In every mall. By every school. Wherever there are hungry kids, we'll open a milk shake shop. And we'll feature the Wicks-Winkle-wow-'em-pow-'em-and-how-'em-drink-it-down-'em-right-now'em—"

"Wicks-Winkle?" Sly interrupted. "Excuse me?"

"Okay, Winkle-Wicks. Where was I? Oh, yeah. 'Right-now'em—' "

"Tony, I don't think you get this. The shake is a Sly Winkle specialty. There's no Wicks about it."

"Wicks!" Sharkey bellowed, making them both jump.

"Like was he cued or what?" Tony murmured, scurrying to the kitchen to find out what Sharkey's latest complaint was.

Sly sighed and stared into his empty glass. This was not the time to think about shake shops. It was decision time for the Dreams. He, Sly Winkle, had to stop BBG and he had to stop him *now*. It was the only way to save California Dreams and win Jenny Garrison's love and admiration.

A man with a mission, Sly raced home to change into a pair of pressed jeans, a black suit jacket, and an eye-blinding red leather tie. Checking his appearance in the mirror, he pointed at his reflection with satisfaction.

"Sly Winkle to the rescue."

His confidence remained high until he walked up the steps of the neon-lit entryway of BBG Records and thought about BBG's attitude. The guy was impossible. How could anyone be so self-centered and shortsighted?

The vacant-looking receptionist acted as if

she'd never seen him before. "Sly Winkle to see Mr. Griffen," Sly told her.

"You got an appointment?"

Sly leaned a hip on her desk. "Just get BBG on the intercom, and we'll go from there."

She made a sound of derision and phoned BBG's secretary. A smug smile crossed her face as she hung up. "You'll have to wait," she told Sly. "Take a seat."

Sly perched on a slick, hot pink chair whose chrome arms and legs were twisted and turned. The thing looked like a mistake and felt like one, too. Checking his watch, Sly realized he was going to miss dinner completely if BBG didn't see him soon.

Ten minutes, he thought to himself as he eyed the receptionist. *Then it's on to diversionary tactics.*

Tiffani hummed a tune as she waited for Drew to pick her up and take her to Sharkey's. She was so glad he'd become a part of her circle of friends. Before Caroline had introduced them, Drew had hung out with his own friends at his own school, but now he was part of her group.

Of course, he wasn't part of the *band* group, which was okay with her as long as it was okay with him, and it seemed to be okay with him. She had to hand it to Jenny for being blunt. Luckily, Drew was such a great guy, it didn't seem to bother him too much.

Drew's rattletrap car wheezed to a stop in front of Tiffani's house. She ran out the front door to meet him. The car's engine popped, hissed, and shuddered.

"Is it going to be all right?" Tiffani asked anxiously.

"Just needs a tune-up. I've gotta get some cash together to fix it."

"Think it'll get us to Sharkey's?"

"Yeah. But after Friday, no more problems."

"After Friday?" Tiffani asked as she slid into the passenger seat beside him. Drew switched on the ignition. The engine ground heavily, slower and slower, finally catching with a choked noise that sounded like a gasp.

Friday? she wondered. A bad feeling came over her. Drew didn't mean the Dreams' recording session with BBG, did he? No, he couldn't. Jenny had told him there was no room for him in the band, and everyone had agreed.

"Jenny writes some of California Dreams' songs, doesn't she?" Drew asked.

"Well, not exactly. But she and Matt have composed some songs together. That new one, for instance," Tiffany answered.

"What new one?"

"It doesn't have a title yet, but I heard Matt say he wants Jenny to sing lead."

"Jenny's really tight with the band even though BBG pushed her out of 'Cross My Heart,'" Drew mused.

Tiffani shrugged and said by way of explanation, "She's Matt's sister."

"Yeah."

Drew narrowed his gaze on the traffic and Tiffani crowded next to him. He didn't squeeze her close as usual. Her brow furrowed. Something was wrong. She just wished she knew what it was.

"Mr. Sly!" BBG greeted Sly with surprise when Sly suddenly zipped inside his office. Sly had sneaked past the receptionist when she'd been inundated with two ringing phones *and* a telephone advertising salesman yapping at her.

"Sorry to interrupt," Sly apologized, "but my schedule's kind of tight and I had to move."

"No problem." BBG took the matter in stride, favoring Sly with a hearty handshake and a few bone-rattling slaps to the back. Coughing, Sly managed to remain on his feet. Between Drew's crushing grip and BBG's body slamming, Sly'd had enough male bonding for a century.

"What can I do you out of?" BBG asked as he swung into his swivel chair and rolled up to his massive desk.

"We need to talk business."

"My favorite subject."

"California Dreams business."

"I like it better and better." BBG grinned, and for reasons Sly didn't want to dwell on, he was reminded of the huge, blue plastic shark curved over Sharkey's doorway.

Rubbing his hands together, Sly paced slowly in front of BBG's desk. "Most decisions that are made aren't perfect for everyone involved. Someone has to compromise. Not everyone gets everything they want."

BBG leaned back in his chair. "I'm listening."

"May I be frank?" Sly asked, stopping directly in front of him.

"By all means. Shoot."

"California Dreams is a well-crafted, beautifully put-together instrument that needs no fine-tuning." Sly was proud of that line. He'd worked on it. "Adding Drew is like throwing perfect pitch off-key."

"Ahh . . ." BBG was thoughtful. "So you and the rest of the Dreams don't want Drew Wylde in the band?"

"Ba-boom," Sly agreed, pointing at BBG.

"You've all discussed this?"

Nodding, Sly added, "I thought it would be

better to get this settled before Friday's video-taping."

"*You* thought it would be better."

"I'm the Dreams' manager," Sly pointed out proudly. "I lead, and they follow."

"I see."

"Drew Wylde doesn't have it," Sly said, driving the point home. This was great. BBG was finally listening!

"You'll be glad to know I've given this matter a lot of thought already." BBG came around to Sly's side of the desk. Sly stepped back. A few more hearty slaps and he'd be hospitalized.

"So Drew's out?" he asked eagerly.

"You're the one who's out, Winkle," BBG announced flatly. "I've found a new manager for the band. Someone else for California Dreams to follow. Someone with clout. Someone who knows the recording industry inside and out: my brother-in-law."

Sly's jaw dropped. "What!"

"So I'll tell you what. You go make sure your friends are there on Friday wearing happy faces. Drew is in and he *stays* in."

One more clap on the back sent Sly reeling from the room. The door slammed behind him. Glancing back, he realized he'd been royally had.

"He called me Winkle," Sly said aloud. The

jerk had known his name all along. And for some reason, that seemed like a bad, bad sign.

Thursday's rehearsal was the last one before the videotaping. Jenny chewed nervously on her lip. Drew was there. He'd been to every rehearsal all week. Though they'd tried to make him understand that he wasn't a part of the Dreams, he'd seemed remarkably dense about the whole thing.

It hadn't helped that Sly had seemed to be on Drew's side. In fact, he'd suggested *Drew* sing lead in Matt's new song. Not a chance!

But worse than that, Tiffani was completely unaware of Drew's true feelings. Clearly he hadn't come clean with her yet, and that made both Jenny and Matt uncomfortable.

Now while Tiffani tuned up, Jenny ran her fingers over the keyboards and tried not to look at Drew, who was reading through the list of their songs. She glanced over at Matt, who was seated at the piano, scribbling notes down in his notebook.

At that moment, Matt looked up and he and Jenny exchanged glances. Jenny couldn't hold his gaze and returned to the keyboards as Tony approached Matt.

"So what are we going to do about—you know." Tony inclined his head in Drew's direction.

"I don't know."

"The guy'll never make the cut," Tony predicted. "He's not even close to video stage. He's awful!"

"BBG liked Drew's image," Matt reminded him.

"Yeah, but wait until he *hears* him! You know what yowling cats sound like? That's our Drew."

"He's not that bad," Sly cut in. He'd been eavesdropping and now felt compelled to comment. "But it'll be okay, anyway. BBG was momentarily dazzled by Drew's muscles," Sly assured them. "Nothing to worry about."

Tony gave a mock shiver. "I hate it when you say things like that. It makes me worry all the more."

"What are you guys talking about?" Jenny called from across the room.

"Nothing," Matt called back. The last thing he wanted was to get into another conversation with Jenny about Drew. She was handling things pretty well, considering, and Matt didn't want to rock the boat.

"I just don't trust him," Matt muttered to Tony and Sly. "There's something about that guy that just doesn't smell right."

"It's all the coconut oil he spreads on those muscles," Sly said, observing Drew's massive chest. Once more the blond monster had shown up half dressed.

"I know what you mean." Tony was serious.

"And doesn't the guy own a shirt?" Sly added, encouraged by Tony's agreement. "Does he show up at school like that?"

"No, I mean, I don't trust Drew, either," Tony clarified. "He's hustling us. And he's using the girls to stay with the band."

"You think so?" Matt asked, not liking the sound of that at all.

"Well, something's weird. He's not hanging around Tiffani as much," Tony pointed out. "There must be some reason."

"Jenny," Matt expelled on a long sigh.

"What?" Sly asked, hoping he hadn't heard right.

"It's because of Jenny. He told her that he and Tiffani weren't right for each other and then made it clear he wanted her."

"Bad news," Tony muttered, glancing guiltily over his shoulder at Tiffani. She caught his look, smiled brightly, and waved.

"Jenny would never fall for a guy like Drew." Sly was positive. "There's not enough candlepower upstairs. Jenny likes brains and talent, and Drew's below average on both."

"I wouldn't be so sure," Matt said dampeningly. "She think he's— nice."

"Who cares about nice?" Sly asked, appalled.

"Oh, man, this sounds like trouble with a capital *T*!" With that, Tony flipped his drumsticks, caught them, and then headed for the raised platform where his drums sat.

The rehearsal was lackluster, and a lot of the songs were off-key. Everyone made mistakes, and by the time they broke up, they were all in a bad mood. To add icing to the cake, Drew hung around Jenny as the Dreams were putting away their equipment, further confusing Tiffani and making Jenny uncomfortable.

Jenny's throat hurt. Feeling someone's stare, she glanced over her shoulder and caught Matt's warning gaze. Shaking her head, she ignored him. She'd said she wouldn't hurt Tiffani—and she wouldn't.

"Jenny and I were just talking about doing some mega-shopping," Tiffani said to the room at large. "We've got to impress Mr. Griffen. And proper costuming is important!"

"Well, I've gotta go flip some Shark burgers," Tony said, easing himself out of the room. "Catch you guys later."

Sly sized up Drew, whose six-foot-plus, bulging frame seemed to fill the room. No way Jenny would go for a guy like that. All brawn and no brain? No way!

Sly's gaze traveled to Jenny's gorgeous face, which was set in rigid lines. She didn't even look like she could stand the guy. But glancing at Matt,

Sly realized there was some kind of silent communication going on between brother and sister.

"No way," Sly muttered under his breath. Still, it might be smart to stick around and see how this thing played out. Jenny was his woman, even if she didn't know it yet.

"I'm getting ready to go," Tiffani told Drew. "You want to head out together?"

"Nah, I can't . . . I've got some things to do." He shifted uncomfortably.

"Okay." Tiffani's voice was sweet and innocent and a bit sad.

Jenny closed her eyes. She wanted to die of guilt. It didn't matter that she hadn't really done anything wrong. The whole thing was terrible.

"Well, Drew, we're kind of closing up shop for today," Matt interjected, "so don't let us hold you up."

"I need to talk to Jenny," Drew threw out.

"Jenny?" Tiffani asked.

Oh, no! Jenny thought, panicked. "If it's about what I said about not needing you in the band, why don't we talk about it later? I—I've got some work to do," she stammered. "Besides, you're still around, right?"

"That's not what I—"

"I think your sound's melding better with us," Matt jumped to the rescue. "Maybe someday we can work out a tune together. Or maybe you'll find another band."

"There's bound to be somebody who'll take you," Sly added encouragingly. "I think."

"I've got to talk to Jenny because we've got a thing going," Drew blurted out loudly. "I might as well be honest. Jenny's my girl."

Holy moley! Jenny could not believe her ears. She froze, mouth open. A terrible silence filled the room. Matt lifted his hand to his eyes as if he felt sick. Sly stared at Jenny in total shock.

"Wha—what?" Tiffani asked in a strained, breathless voice.

"I'm sorry, Tiffani," Drew said seriously. "It's over. I didn't know how to tell you, so I just had to say it."

The blood drained from Tiffani's face. "I don't believe you. Jenny would never—" She broke off, turning to Jenny for help. When she saw Jenny's guilt-stricken face, she made a strangled sound.

Without another word, she ran out of the garage.

Chapter 11

"**N**ice going, Einstein!" Sly yelled at Drew. "Way to use those broad, empty spaces inside your skull!"

"You're not exactly Mr. Sensitivity yourself," Jenny snapped at Sly, shaken. "Excuse me." She started after Tiffani.

"Wait." Drew held her shoulders, stopping her.

Matt stepped forward. "Take your hands off her."

"Give Tiffani some time," Drew said to Jenny. "I know it was a shock. I did it badly. I'm sorry."

Jenny didn't know what to do with him. She stared at him helplessly, which earned her a snort from Sly.

"What is it about this guy?" Sly demanded. "He's a total jerk! The way he just treated Tiffani proves it!"

Jenny ran past Drew, Sly, and Matt and chased after Tiffani, but Tiffani was gone by the time she got to the driveway. Crushed, Jenny slumped against the side of the garage.

Drew appeared. "Can I talk to you?"

"Not now, Drew."

Jenny stumbled toward the house and the safety of her bedroom. Hugging a pillow to her chest, she tried to sort out her feelings, but there was no way to make any kind of sense of anything.

And tomorrow's the video shoot, she thought miserably. She wanted to kill Drew for his lousy timing.

Jenny tried dialing Tiffani's number, but the answering machine picked up. She left a message for Tiffani to call her, but by ten o'clock that night she still hadn't heard from her.

What if Tiffani doesn't show up tomorrow? Jenny worried as she tried to fall asleep that night.

Tension filled the air as the Dreams assembled at BBG Records for their recording and videotaping Friday afternoon. Jenny was so wound up, she jumped at every little noise. Tiffani was late, or maybe a purposeful no-show, but Drew was smack-dab in the center spotlight.

This time he had worn a shirt, though not one button had seen a buttonhole. His shells were on, and his blond hair hung like a mane to his shoulders.

Jenny sniffed. He was wearing coconut oil!

Anger hardened in a knot inside her. Who did he think he was? Nice? She'd thought he was *nice*? How could he have done that to Tiffani? What was his angle, really? Now that she thought about it, she didn't buy this whole "you're my girl" act. Had he used her to dump Tiffani? It sure felt that way.

"You did tell BBG we don't want Drew, right?" Matt questioned Sly.

Sly glanced at Drew. "Is he smirking? Is that a smirk on his face?"

"Sly!"

"I told you, I laid out our feelings to BBG. He said he'd give the matter some thought."

"But Drew is here," Matt pointed out. "In our faces."

"Did I invite him? No. Did you invite him? No. Did Jenny invite him? No. He invited himself."

"What if Tiffani doesn't show?" Matt worried, his gaze skating over Tony, who was practicing at his drum set, to Jenny, who looked like a storm cloud had settled over her head.

"She'll be here," Sly said, though his voice lacked conviction. "She'll definitely be here."

At that moment, BBG and his red-haired companion showed up. "Okay, run through that song that Jenny-babe sang last week."

" 'Cross My Heart,' " Matt reminded him as he took his place with the band. He glanced down the line to Jenny, who was studiously ignoring Drew.

"Where's the blond chick?" BBG demanded.

"She'll be here," Jenny said tightly. "We need to practice before we record, anyway. She'll be here any minute."

"Fine. Fine. But, Jenny . . ." BBG crooked his finger, inviting her to have a little heart-to-heart.

"If you've got something to say about the band, just say it." Jenny stayed where she was. "We don't have any secrets."

BBG slid her a long look. "Okay. Jenny-babe, you've got a great voice. A fabulous voice. But like I said before, we're too heavy on female vocals. I'm taking you out of the video."

"What?" Matt screeched, infuriated.

"Now, wait just a darn minute!" Sly stalked over to BBG. "You can't cut out Jenny. We won't stand for it."

"As I recall, you're no longer manager of this band," BBG said with a snarl. "Ray!" He snapped his fingers, and the red-haired man leaped to attention. "This is my brother-in-law, Raymond Bentley. He's the band's manager."

"Jenny stays in the video, Ray," Matt snarled

right back. "And Sly's still our manager!"

"That's right!" Tony slammed his drumsticks down with a bang.

"It's all right, guys." Jenny stepped away from the keyboards and to the back of the room, arms folded over her chest to keep herself from breaking into some embarrassing, hysterical fit. She was not going to cry. Uh-uh. She'd rather die than have BBG and Drew see her reduced to tears. Curling her nails into her palms, she set her jaw and prepared to be "big" about this.

"I thought you'd knock Tiffani out," Drew said. "Jenny's Matt's sister."

BBG gave him a "who cares?" look. "Tiffani's backup on this song. I needed to remove the lead."

"We're not going to do it without Jenny," Matt declared.

"Then you're not going to do it at all!" BBG returned. "You've got fifteen minutes. When I come back, give me your decision. Talk to them, Ray," he ordered as he strode from the room.

The red-haired man glanced from Matt to Tony to Drew. He ignored Jenny altogether. Clearing his throat, he said, "Don't blow this chance." Then he chased after BBG.

Matt, Tony, and Sly started arguing loudly. Jenny wanted to clap her hands over her ears, but instead she concentrated her fury on BBG. And what was that comment that Drew had made all about? He'd expected either her or Tiffani to be dumped?

The door opened, and Tiffani walked in quietly. She didn't look at anyone as she started setting up.

"Hi, Tiff," Matt greeted her.

"Hi," she said.

"Tiffani, could I talk to you?" Jenny asked.

Tiffani looked like she wanted to say no, but in the end she agreed, and she and Jenny went out to the hallway. There was an awkward moment; then Jenny heaved a huge sigh.

"Tiff, I'm not Drew's girl. He lied."

Tiffani's golden brown eyes looked up hopefully at Jenny. She wanted to believe her. "But why would Drew say that?"

"I don't know." She paced around. "Maybe I do," she admitted a moment later. "I might have given him the wrong idea."

"What do you mean?"

"Oh, Tiffani . . . ," Jenny groaned. Even though she hadn't acted on her feelings, she wasn't completely blameless. "I guess I sent out the wrong vibes. I was attracted to Drew. I mean, he's different than the guys I usually date."

"You were attracted to him."

"Sort of. But I wasn't seeing Drew," Jenny assured her. "Tiffani, no matter how I felt, I could never do that to you!"

129

"But you were attracted to him," she repeated, shifting her weight from one sandaled foot to the other. Tiffani was in a short, white wraparound skirt and Hawaiian-print tie-front blouse over a hot pink bikini top.

Jenny's gaze skated over her own outfit: blue shorts, white crocheted shell over a white tank top, and sneakers. They hadn't managed their mega-shopping trip, so they'd both worn beachwear to the taping.

Only now Jenny wouldn't be in the video.

"Maybe I just wanted a boyfriend," Jenny admitted, forced to do a little soul-searching. "It's been tough ever since Sean left, and seeing you with Drew . . . I don't know."

"But Drew's not even your type," Tiffani argued, shaking her blond tresses. "He's big and muscular and gentle and sweet."

"He's got green eyes like Sean's." Jenny grimaced. "And I don't know about that gentle and sweet part."

Tiffani blinked. "You don't?"

"Look at the way he treated you! He broke up with you in the worst possible way."

Tiffani thought that over. "Maybe he had to do it that way," she said in a small voice. "I mean, he wanted you to know how he felt. He'd kind of let me know in little ways that it was over, but I didn't really get it."

"That's no excuse for hurting you."

Tiffani looked like she might cry, but then she blinked rapidly several times and finally managed a faint smile. "So, what are you going to do?"

"Me? Nothing."

"I thought Drew and I were soul mates, but I guess he really likes you," Tiffani struggled to get out. "If you feel the same, I don't want to be the reason you two don't get together."

"No, Tiffani. No, no, no." Jenny shook her head. "I don't want Drew."

"But he wants you."

Something was bothering Jenny. Something Tiffani had said earlier. She couldn't quite think what it was. It was on the tip of her tongue, and she thought she had it when Sly pushed open the recording room door.

"They're back," he sang in a great imitation of the little girl in *Poltergeist*.

"Guess we'd better go shoot that video." Tiffani smiled at Jenny. "I'm sorry I was so upset yesterday. I should've called you back."

"Don't worry about it. You had a right to be upset."

"Is Drew in the video?" Tiffani asked suddenly.

"Uh, yeah, he is."

"For 'Cross My Heart'? What part's he singing?"

"Tiffani! Jenny! Come on!" Sly gestured furiously at them to come back into the studio.

"Actually, he's singing mine," Jenny informed her.

"Well?" BBG asked, arms crossed over his black suit.

"You can't cut Jenny out!" Tiffani declared. "We won't stand for it, will we?" She turned to Tony and Matt, who immediately concurred.

"That's your answer?" BBG asked intently.

"Wait, wait!" Jenny lifted her palms for them to stop. "The Dreams will record the song and shoot the video."

"No, Jenny, it's not fair," Matt protested. Tony, Tiffani, and Sly echoed his sentiment. Drew remarkably remained quiet as if afraid to become embroiled in this argument.

"It's just one video," Jenny told them. "When we all become rich and famous, I'll get my shot along with the rest of you."

"Good girl!" BBG clapped his hands together. "Now come on. Let's get rolling. Drew, you're on. Let's hear what you've got."

BBG graciously allowed Jenny access to the control room, and she sat to one side with Sly as the new California Dreams ran through take after take of "Cross My Heart." Jenny didn't much care for the new sound. Maybe it was sour grapes, but she

132

didn't think the song had nearly the same resonance as when she'd sung lead.

"Not too good, huh?" Sly whispered in her ear.

"For once, we agree completely." Jenny felt an arm steal across her back. She jerked a glance to her left and saw Sly's hand curve possessively around her shoulder. "Not that completely," she hissed, and with a sigh Sly removed his arm.

On the last note of the song, BBG called through the microphone, "That's great, guys and gals. I'm bringing in the video team."

"Already?" Jenny gasped. "It was so—mediocre! The Dreams can do much better."

"I don't have all day." BBG shrugged.

Jenny backed off, and Sly, seeing his chance to redeem himself, stepped up to the plate. "Drew's not quite in sync, BBG. In fact, I'm not sure he'll ever be. Now, Jenny here—"

"Mr. Sly, you're not the band's manager," BBG reminded him. "In fact, your presence here is undermining Ray's authority."

Sly glanced at Ray, who looked to BBG for guidance.

"We never agreed to change managers!" Jenny spoke up heatedly.

Ignoring her, BBG kept his gaze trained on Sly. "I'm afraid I'm going to have to ask you to leave. As of this moment, your association with my band has been terminated."

Chapter 12

Matt unstrapped his guitar and eased the kinks out of his back. Bringing in the video team! Was BBG crazy? "We're not even close to right yet," he muttered.

Drew overheard. "I thought it was great. Did you see that little move I made with my head?" He demonstrated by tossing back his blond hair and curling his lip.

"The song's about true love, Drew," Matt pointed out.

"Yeah? So?"

Matt glanced back at Tony for help. "I don't know about you, man," Tony explained, "but I try not to snarl when I'm telling my girl how I feel. It's kind of a turnoff."

"Women are funny that way," Matt added, smothering a smile.

"You never snarled when we were together," Tiffani pointed out. Drew sent her a sharp look, but she refused to meet his gaze.

The door opened. "Here comes the bossman," Tony murmured as BBG strode into the room, followed by Ray. The door started to swing shut, but Jenny caught it and she and Sly entered the room. Jenny strode forward, ready to spit nails.

"We're setting up," BBG said. "But this surf look has got to go. We've shot some videos with black leather and silver studs. The costume designer will be here soon to fit you all."

"Black leather and silver studs!" Jenny stopped short in midstride. "Are you kidding?"

BBG turned to her in irritation, but then his brow smoothed and he draped an arm over her shoulder, steering her toward the side of the room. "Jenny-babe, while your input is invaluable, I don't have a lot of time to play games. Let me do my job, and you just wait patiently. Okay?"

Sly sidled up to her as BBG turned back to the band. Before he could say anything, Jenny muttered intensely, "He can't fire you. We won't have it! He's crazy!"

"Shhh. While I appreciate the support, let's not blow this," Sly told her. He wasn't worried.

Well, he was sort of worried. But with the Dreams on his side, there wasn't a lot BBG could do about dumping him.

After all, the contracts weren't signed yet. . . .

As if reading Sly's thoughts, BBG snapped his fingers. "Bring those contracts down, Ray."

Ray raced out to meet BBG's demands. Tony, Matt, and Tiffani stared at BBG with varying degrees of distrust. Drew's eyes were all over Tiffani.

What gives? Jenny thought, her suspicions aroused.

"This ought to be interesting," Sly predicted as the costume designer, who looked like something from a nightmare, showed up carrying a load of black leather. She dumped the pile of clothes at Drew's feet and announced, "I don't know if I've got anything to fit the big guy."

"We'll figure it out," BBG said.

"Really interesting," Jenny agreed slowly.

Two hours later, the video team was assembled and Tony, Matt, Tiffani, and Drew were sweating under hot lights and black leather. Tiffani wore a black leather top about a size too small and hip-hugging, skintight pants encircled with silver chains. BBG had ordered scarlet lipstick, and the color had washed out Tiffani's already light skin. Now she looked anemic. However, no amount of costuming could take away from her innate sweetness and goodness. Instead of appearing tough and hard, she merely seemed childlike and confused.

Matt and Tony wore black leather jackets with silver studs and their own washed-out jeans. They almost looked respectable. Drew, however, had once again opted out of his shirt. Since the designer couldn't fit him, he'd been given a set of black leather chaps trimmed with slinky, silver fringe. The shell necklace had been replaced with a black leather choker encrusted with pointed studs.

"That looks like a bulldog collar," Sly remarked to Jenny.

"Why do I get the feeling Drew likes it?" she asked, her opinion of him sinking still lower.

"Because he's snarling?"

BBG examined the setup. "Perfect!" he declared. "Let's start."

"May I point out something about the mood of this song?" Matt asked.

"No," BBG answered. "Let's roll."

Without further ado, the cameras moved in close, the music started, and Drew and the remaining Dreams sang "Cross My Heart." Jenny didn't know which was worse: the sound or the scene.

She and Sly looked at each other.

"Interesting," Sly said.

"Very," Jenny agreed with a smile. For a moment, one shining instant, she saw the real Sylvester Winkle, a cute guy with a lot of charm.

"Are those eyes begging for a kiss?" he asked, lifting one brow and smiling smugly.

Poof! The instant was over. Reality check. "Get a life," she muttered, and walked to the opposite corner of the room.

"So what did you think?" Tiffani asked Jenny afterward. She still wore her black leather outfit, but she'd rubbed off the lipstick.

"Well . . ." Jenny didn't want to sound like a wet blanket, but honesty was generally the best policy.

"Don't answer." Matt sighed heavily. "It was pure garbage and we all know it. We needed you, Jenny. That—and a fashion transfusion."

Jenny smiled, thrilled with Matt's support. Everyone seemed to agree with him. Well, almost everyone.

Drew snorted. "What are you talking about? It was awesome!"

"Awesomely rotten," Tony said. "We *do* need you, Jenny."

"There's something missing without you," Tiffani agreed.

"Thanks," Jenny murmured. Feeling the weight of Drew's stare, she met his gaze, but instead of agreeing with the others, he turned to Tiffani.

"You were great," he told her.

Tiffani uttered a short laugh. "Oh, yeah, sure.

Like it would have made a big difference if I was there or not. Jenny's the one that—"

"Our voices melded," he interrupted earnestly. "Yours and mine."

"Drew!" For once in her life, Tiffani looked truly annoyed. "See you in a bit, guys," she added. "I'm going to change."

"Could we talk?" Drew inserted quickly as she turned away. "I need to say some things. Apologize for how I acted."

Jenny swept in a startled breath. What was this?

"I smell a rat," Matt singsonged softly.

Tiffani narrowed her gaze on Drew. "I don't think I want to talk," she said, and then stalked away, teetering a bit on the ultra-high heels she'd been allotted.

"I'm sorry!" he yelled. "It was all a mistake."

"I get it now." Jenny's voice was cold. "You only wanted me when you thought I was more important to the band than Tiffani was!"

Drew pretended not to hear her. "Tiffani!" he called, starting after her. Jenny grabbed his elbow and yanked him back.

"That's how you met her in the first place, isn't it? You forced a meeting! Caroline Newsome told you Tiffani was a part of the Dreams and you decided to move in. It was a great act. Drew Wylde, the sweet-tempered, slow-thinking nice guy who wouldn't hurt a fly. But all the time, those wheels were turning inside your head."

"Jenny, Jenny, Jenny." Drew's tone was patronizing.

"You had a hidden agenda all along," Matt declared in amazement. "Didn't you?"

"So all I wanted was to be in a band, okay?" Drew tossed back. "Is that a crime?"

"A crime of the heart, man," Tony piped in, furious, "when you play with people's feelings!"

"You never cared about Tiffani at all." Jenny shook her head in disbelief. "You never cared about anyone but yourself."

"Is that true, Drew?"

Tiffani's voice sounded from the dim recesses at the back of the room. Jenny realized Tiffani had opened the door to leave, but their argument had stopped her. She'd heard every comment.

"Tiffani . . ." Drew started to sweat.

She wobbled back over to them, her chin stuck out stubbornly. "You said we were soul mates," she whispered.

Jenny couldn't believe it! That's what she'd almost remembered earlier when she and Tiffani were talking. "He told *you* that you were soul mates? He used the same line on me. Actually, though, he didn't even get it right. He said we were soul friends!"

Tiffani gasped. "That's what he said to me!"

"Girls, girls." Drew waved them off dismissively. "I like you both. I just couldn't decide."

"Save me," Jenny muttered.

"You are one slimeball," Tony muttered.

"Yeah, well, I'm not exactly thrilled to be with you losers, either!" Drew shot back, showing his true stripes at last. "But we're stuck with each other, so get used to it!"

"You used us to claw your way up the ladder of success," Matt declared. "You used Tiffani and then you used Jenny!"

"You trampled on our love in the name of ambition," Tiffani put in. "Take a hike, buster. Right over Lovers' Leap!"

Jenny, Matt, and Tony cheered, and Sly clapped in approval.

Drew's face darkened brick red. "I'm the best thing your stupid garage band's got! The *only* thing. Without me, BBG would pull the plug on you guys."

"BBG was set to use us before you ever came along," Sly reminded him. "So why don't you go back to the jungle where you belong."

"You! You're not even manager anymore," Drew snarled, stomping away.

"I'm sorry," Tiffani said after the door had banged shut behind him. "This is all my fault."

"It is not," Jenny told her. "He suckered me in, too."

"What an idiot. He really thinks we'd dump Sly for Ray just because BBG told us to?" Matt made a sound of disgust.

Jenny glanced at Sly, who cleared his throat and grimaced. "Actually, BBG did give me the old ax."

"But he can't do that!" Jenny's eyes flashed fire. "Sly's the manager of California Dreams and that's that. We make the decisions, not BBG or anybody else."

Sly grinned at her. "I'm touched."

"I'm serious, Sly! Nobody makes those kind of changes without consulting us. We've got to stand up for ourselves now or BBG will run right over us. I say that we don't sign those contracts unless Sly's written in as our manager."

Matt, Tony, Jenny, and Tiffani slapped each other "five" on the agreement. Sly couldn't help feeling a bit humbled by his friends' support. But this was his chance with Jenny. Now. While she was feeling so warm and protective.

"I really appreciate what you said," he told Jenny softly.

Jenny shrugged, slightly embarrassed. "Maybe you're not as big a lowlife as I thought you were. The cowinners of that award are Drew and BBG."

"Gee, what a rave review."

Jenny laughed. "Don't let it go to your head."

"Okay . . . but how about we seal the deal on a date together. You and me?"

Trapped! Jenny looked to Matt for support. Matt held up his hands in surrender and backed away. Ditto for Tony and Tiffani.

Jenny gazed assessingly at Sly. Even though he had some serious character flaws, he was her friend. And after this fiasco with Drew, she seriously needed her friends.

"There would have to be a few conditions," she said slowly.

"Name them!" Sly declared eagerly.

"The rest of the Dreams have to go with us."

"What? No!"

"And we can only see each other between the hours of six and ten—in the morning."

"Jenny!"

"And it's got to be during a quarter moon, in the springtime, when it's snowing."

"In California?" Sly demanded. Jenny's eyes sparkled with humor. "Okay, okay, I give up," he conceded. "For now. But one day, it's you and me, kid," he told her.

"Sure, Sly." Jenny shook her head.

With the assurance of a conquering hero, BBG banged back through the door, a sheaf of papers in his hands. On his heels came Ray and a grinning Drew.

"Uh-oh," Matt said, and the rest of the

143

Dreams and Sly gathered around him.

"It's time we finalized this," BBG broke right in. "And guess what, I've got a great idea."

They all stood silently. This couldn't be good news.

Moments later, they learned how bad it really was.

BBG held out his arms as if they were all his children and he wanted to give them a collective hug. "I've come up with a new name for the group. Try this on for size: the Drew Wylde Band!"

Everyone gasped. Matt blinked several times. "Mr. Griffen, you've put a lot of time and effort into the Dreams, but this new image"—his gaze flicked toward Drew—"isn't what we're about. Drew's not a part of our band. Jenny is. We need things back the way they were if we're going to sign with BBG Records."

"Are you crazy?" Drew vehemently shook his blond locks.

"It's not up to Drew. It's up to us," Matt said sternly. "Drew can find a new band. He's not part of California Dreams."

BBG glanced at their faces one by one. Apparently, he must have seen how determined they were because he actually seemed to consider their demands. Finally, he drew in a breath. "Well, kids, I'm sorry this didn't work out." With that, he ripped up the contracts and tossed them to the ground.

Everyone stared in amazement at the bits of floating paper.

"Me, too," Matt murmured with regret.

"But on to new business," BBG added brightly. "*Adios,* Dreams. I'm going to make Drew a star!"

With that, he and Drew shook hands and clapped each other on the back, nearly knocking each other over as they congratulated themselves on their new partnership. They walked out together.

"What just happened?" Sly asked, stunned.

"The inevitable," Matt answered, resigned. "The inevitable."

Three weeks later, Tony sighed as he scratched the tropical-whopical shake from Sharkey's menu. "No one'll even try it," he complained to Sly, Matt, Jenny, and Tiffani, who were in the midst of Shark burgers and fries.

"I've got one." Sly pointed to his glass.

"One isn't enough!" Tony sighed. "Guess I'll have to come up with a new method of marketing or else find a new product."

"How's it going with Sharkey these days?" Matt asked.

"About the same," Tony admitted.

Tiffani was listening to a portable radio through a set of headphones. "Take off those headphones so we can all hear," Jenny suggested. "I don't want to waste my quarters feeding the jukebox."

Tiffani removed the headphones, and they all listened to the top-forty hits.

"We could've been big," Sly said for about the hundredth time since BBG had cut them loose. "Maybe we should have hung in there."

"And have Ray as manager and Drew as lead?" Jenny reminded him.

"I keep forgetting the negatives," Sly admitted.

"Are you guys ready to set up?" Tiffani asked them.

Matt nodded as he got up from the table. "Tell me again what Sharkey's paying us for tonight's gig," he said to Sly.

"It hasn't been completely worked out yet," Sly admitted.

Matt groaned and headed for Sharkey's corner stage. "I was afraid of that."

Matt didn't really care. It was just great to be playing with Tony, Tiffani, *and* Jenny again. As soon as Tony's shift was over, he would join them.

"Wicks!" Sharkey yelled, and Tony, who was luckily in the midst of taking an order, gazed at him expectantly as he strode across the restaurant floor.

"Who screwed up this order?" he demanded, waving an order slip in front of Tony's nose.

Tony glanced at the slip. "That's Carrie's order."

Sharkey snatched it back, tried to read Carrie's indecipherable scrawl, and then snorted and started back to the kitchen.

"Hey, Sharkey," Tony called after him. "I've been doing some figuring on my income per order. Since I only come in after school, I work less hours than your full-timers."

"So?"

"But I work the busiest hours of the day, so I have to be filling more orders per hour than the people who're here all day. You see, it's all a matter of mathematics," Tony added, warming to his theme. "So it appears your theory's all wet. I'm making more money for you than anybody else is."

Sharkey looked like he was about to explode. Tiffani put her fingers in her ears as if actually expecting it to happen.

Jenny grinned hugely as Sharkey muttered something under his breath and bellowed at Carrie.

"Good going, Tony," Jenny said as he took off his Sharkey's baseball shirt and threw on a black jacket. "What was he saying before he yelled at Carrie?"

"Something about kids being too smart today." Tony chuckled and Jenny joined in.

"Hey!" Sly called from the table, holding up Tiffani's portable stereo. "Listen to this!" He turned up the dial.

"*. . . and now, the incomparable Drew Wylde Band!*" the announcer yelled feverishly.

Sly brought the portable stereo over to the stage. All of the Dreams listened to Drew belt out a song called "Terminal."

"It's not bad," Matt said after a few moments.

"No . . . ," Jenny agreed a bit unwillingly.

"You can tell it's Drew, sort of," Tiffani tried hard to sound positive.

"It's got a decent beat," Tony struggled.

"Are you guys nuts?" Sly demanded. "It's tinny and shallow and monotonous. And it reminds me of another band."

Tony, Matt, Tiffani, and Jenny looked at each other and started laughing. "The Breathsprays!" they chorused together.

"Another BBG Records discovery," Matt added, laughing so hard he could scarcely catch his breath. "Come on, guys, let's hit my new song."

"Hey, man, what's the title again?" Tony asked as he seated himself behind his drum set.

" 'Who Can You Trust?' " Jenny answered for him. "And the lyrics kind of say it all: You can trust your friends."

She and Tiffani shared a look of understanding. Tony nodded, liking the sound of that. Matt counted off the start of the song, and Sly sat back, clasping his hands behind his head and wondering if he could play on this friendship angle to finally win Jenny Garrison, heart and soul.

Perfect Harmony

Romance is everywhere! Pacific Coast High's school newspaper started a "personals" column, and everyone who is anyone is writing in – searching for the PERFECT date!

But while all his friends are in search of love, Matt's love life is in trouble. Randi Jo is tired of playing second fiddle to California Dreams, and when an adorable new DJ named Chloe comes into Matt's life, things get too hot to handle. Meanwhile, Jenny spotted Sean in a red Corvette with a gorgeous girl AND he stood her up on a date!

Will Matt be able to resist Chloe's irresistible smile? And is Sean seeing another girl behind Jenny's back? Find out when you read *Perfect Harmony*, the new novel about California Dreams – the hottest band around!

Playing for Keeps

Excitement is in the air! The Redondo Beach Club bash is Saturday night and California Dreams hopes to play at it. But when rival band Solar Energy is chosen to play instead of California Dreams, Matt, Jenny, and the rest of the band are heart-broken. Things go from bad to worse when Jenny falls for the gorgeous hunk Sean Flynn – Solar Energy's lead singer!

Meanwhile, Sly is convinced that all California Dreams really needs is a professionally recorded demo tape. So he pulls some big-time strings and lands them time with a real, live recording studio.

But is it too late? Will Jenny leave California Dreams to sing with her new love in Solar Energy? Find out when you read *Playing for Keeps*, the new novel about California Dreams – the hottest band around!

ONE WILD WEEKEND

Zack's in big trouble. Not only did he trash someone's motorcycle, but that someone is Denny Vane, Bayside High's most intimidating bad-boy.

Meanwhile, Lisa's job at the hospital takes a turn for the better when a patient offers her (and her friends)) his cabin in the mountains for a weekend. And when Zack hears about it, he's delighted – what better place to escape Denny Vane than the mountains!

But when Zack and the gang head for the hills for romance and excitement, things get a little complicated. Kelly, Lisa, and Jessie fall head over heels for three gorgeous Italians, and Zack finds himself in more trouble than ever!

Will Denny Vane discover just who did total his beloved bike? And will Kelly and Jessie leave their Bayside boys behind for their charming, European hunks? Find out what ahppens when you read One Wild Weekend, the hot new novel about the "Saved by the Bell" gang.

GIRLS' NIGHT OUT

It's girls' night out and that spells trouble for Zack, Slater, and Screech.

Jessie is furious with Slater over his flirtations with georgeous Tamara Talbot. But when Slater tells Jessie she could learn a few things from a girl like Tamara, Jessie really loses her cool – and things at Bayside High become downright combustible!

It's love at first sight when Jessie meets surfer-hunk Thunder Thorpe, but when Thunder's ex-girlfriend, Star, keeps showing up, Kelly and Lisa aren't so sure. Jessie's falling in with the wrong crowd, but what can the rest of the gang do to help her?

Unless Zack comes up with a fool-proof plan right away, Jessie might just kiss Slater good-bye forever! Find out what happens when you read *Girl's Night Out*, the hot new novel about the "Saved by the Bell" gang.

HOW TO ORDER YOUR SAVED BY THE BELL
AND CALIFORNIA DREAMS BOOKS FROM BOXTREE